HANNAH'S ANGEL

SHARON SROCK

Cari
Merry Christmas!
Sharon

For Chase Yates. Always the tender hearted one. There are no words to tell you how proud I am of the man you've become. I love you!
For the Lord God is a sun and shield: the Lord will give grace and glory: no good thing will He withhold from them that walk uprightly. Psalms 84:11

ACKNOWLEDGMENTS

For my Father in Heaven. They would be no story without your leading. Thank you for endurance and words. I hope I strung them together in a way that pleases you.

And even then...the words would be lost without the people who read, edit, advise, and pray. You have my undying gratitude every single day!

1

The angel hovered on an updraft of warm air for several seconds before landing face down in a basket of french fries. Terri Evans yanked it out of the ketchup and wiped red sauce from the pristine white wings. She looked up to the second level of the mall. From their table in the food court, the large Christmas tree, hung with similar paper angels, was barely visible.

"What have you got there?" Callie asked.

"Looks like one of the angels from the tree upstairs," Terri said. "It must have blown free or gotten knocked loose." She pushed her food aside to better study the renegade angel and flipped it over with a frown. The information written on the back was unusually sparse. *Hannah Price, Garfield OK.* Weird. She passed the angel across the table to Karla McAlister. "Take a look."

Karla took the ornament. Pam Lake and Callie Stillman twisted in their chairs to read over her shoulder. The sight of her three best friends huddled together brought a smile to Terri's face. Karla, her silver hair styled in an attractive bob, her green eyes filled with sixty-five years of wisdom. Callie, a short, blond, blue-eyed grandmother whose temperament could change from scolding to compassionate in half a heartbeat. And Pam, a dark haired beauty who'd just celebrated her forty-sixth birthday but could pass for thirty. They represented a combination of kindness, insight, and strength that always amazed Terri. Together she was pretty sure they could clear up a rainy day if the situation called for it.

Pam's perfectly arched brows rose over her brown eyes. "That's odd. Just a name and town. No age, sizes, or wish list."

Terri glanced at the stack of paper ornaments resting in front of each of them. They'd taken six apiece. She and her three friends had plucked those from the tree earlier in the day before coming down here to eat lunch and make some notes in anticipation of their annual shopping spree.

Terri had begun the Christmas Angel tradition for herself several years ago, before she'd married and grown a family of her own. Back then, she'd been the only one of the four friends still single. With no kids to dote on, the opportunity to play Santa for a handful of needy children served to fill a bit of the void. The practice quickly spread to her three friends, and now each year on the first Saturday in December, they came together and selected six names apiece from the tree. In dozens of Christmas angels and the kids they represented, this was the first time she'd seen one so incomplete. How could you shop for gifts with so little information to go on?

She held her hand out when her friends looked up,

obviously as puzzled as she was. "Let me have it. The tree is just across from the toy store. We'll hang it back up for someone else to harvest."

Keep it.

Terri shrugged the errant thought aside as she gathered her trash and folded her six angels inside her note pad. She'd take every one on the tree if she could. But she had her quota for this year.

The four friends headed for the escalator that would take them back to the second level. A moment later, Terri secured the angel to a branch of the tree with its attached ribbon. She tilted her head. *That's weird too. All of the others have red or green ribbons. Why is this one white?* She brushed the question aside, blew hard, and fanned it with her hand in an effort to dislodge it. Hannah's angel fluttered but clung tight to its branch. Satisfied with its stability and confident that someone would pluck it soon—for all the good it would do them—Terri crossed to the toy store where the others waited. She surveyed the glittering stacks of potential gifts, rubbed her hands together, and grabbed a cart. "Come on. This is my favorite part."

Hannah's angel faded from Terri's thoughts as she pushed the basket through narrow aisles crowded with Christmas shoppers. There were four girls and two boys on her list this year. She studied dolls and stuffed animals, tested remote control cars, and read the warnings and specifications on an assortment of skateboards before adding one to the cart. When she rounded the final counter she saw her friends huddled at the end of the checkout line.

Karla's silver hair glinted under the florescent lights as she shook her head to a question Terri hadn't heard.

Callie's face held a serious look of suspicion, while Pam gestured at something in Karla's hand. Terri hurried over. "What's wrong?" she whispered.

"I'm not sure," Karla answered. "I was going through my notes to make sure I had everything and..." She shook her head and held out her hand to Terri. "Look what I found tucked inside my notebook."

Terri lowered her eyes to Karla's hand and felt her breath catch in her throat. Hannah's angel stared up at her, ketchup stain and all. "You snuck out and picked that back off the tree."

Karla shook her head. "That seems to be the general consensus, but"—she sketched an X across her heart—"I haven't been out of the store."

"Then how—?"

"Oh good grief, ladies, get a clue," Pam said. "Someone's playing a joke on us and we're falling for it. Where was your notebook?"

Karla motioned to her cart. "I left it in the cart so I wouldn't have to dig for it every time I wanted to check something off."

"Well there you go. You know what pranksters our husbands are." Pam waved at the bustling throng of shoppers out on the walkway. "I'll bet they're all four lurking out there somewhere. They saw us put the angel back on the tree and figured they had a chance to get our goats. I, for one, refuse to give them the satisfaction." She held out her hand. "Give me that thing and watch my purse." Pam left her basket and marched out of the store.

They watched as the angel was secured to the tree a third time. There were grins all around as Pam tugged on it and brushed against it to insure its firm attachment to the tree. Obviously satisfied, she dusted her hands together and returned to her friends. "Ok, ladies. Let's finish up in here. We have clothing stores to visit."

They had a formula they used for each name they drew. A toy, an outfit, and a winter coat with matching hat and gloves. Half a dozen stores later, Terri stood to the side while Callie paid for her final purchase, a purple hooded jacket for a teenage girl on her list. Callie dug in her purse. "Anyone got extra pennies. I really don't want to break a twenty for three cents."

Pam reached into her basket and pulled out the sweater she'd abandoned earlier. "I do. I've been dropping change in my pockets all afternoon. What the..." She pulled her hand out of her pocket. She had pennies all right. Pennies wrapped up in a winkled paper angel. "I don't believe this."

The harried sales clerk frowned as the four friends gathered around Pam.

Karla laughed. "They're persistent, you have to give them that."

Pam spread the angel out on the counter and pointed to the red stain on the wing. "Yep, same angel." Her eyes roamed the crowded store and the corridor beyond. "They're good. I haven't seen a hint that they're following us. Have any of you?"

Headshakes all around.

Callie plucked pennies and the angel out of Pam's hand, paid for her purchases, and headed out of the store.

"Back to the tree?" Terri asked.

"Nope. Whoever's doing this has had their fun, but

enough is enough." Callie paused in the middle of the walkway next to a trash can.

Terri frowned at her friend. "Callie, you can't throw it away. Hannah—"

"Hannah what?" Callie asked. "You were the one who noticed how incomplete the information is. If someone picked it off the tree, they wouldn't be able to do anything with it. This is someone's idea of a practical joke." Her blue eyes met each of theirs in turn. "Agreed?"

Pam and Karla nodded their heads while Terri hesitated. She really could see the guys messing with them. If any of the ladies gave any indication of being spooked, it would be Easter before their husbands let them live it down. But...how had the angel landed in her fries in the first place? The men were good, but were they that good? Callie sent her a questioning look. Terri's shoulders lifted, and a sigh puffed out her cheeks, there wasn't another logical explanation. "Agreed."

"Great." Callie balled the offending paper up and tossed it in the can. "Joke over. Let's get all this stuff out to our cars. Last stop of the day, Chili Mac's for dessert and coffee, my treat."

Terri trailed her three friends towards the exit, but she couldn't keep herself from looking over her shoulder at the trash can in the distance. She couldn't ignore the small niggle of doubt, *guilt,* at the discarded angel or the muffled *keep it* that echoed in her heart.

The restaurant was as packed as the stores had been, but the lure of warm chocolate cake topped with vanilla ice cream proved to be a strong incentive for patience. When presented with dessert menus, eyes quickly grew bigger than stomachs.

Terri pushed her half-eaten dessert away, stuffed but unable to resist the urge to swipe her finger through the chocolate that remained on the plate. "If I eat another bite, I'll pop."

Karla stuck her spoon in Terri's leftover mound of ice cream and helped herself to a bite with a wicked grin. "Wimp."

Callie pulled out her wallet. "The perfect way to end a perfect day. Good friends, shopping, and chocolate." She gave a startled squeak and dropped her wallet on the table. Her pointed finger drew everyone's eyes to the piece of paper that rested between the leather folds.

Pam lifted it and slowly spread it out in the center of the table. *Hannah Price, Garfield OK.* Four puzzled pair of eyes stared down at the bedraggled angel.

"How are they doing this?" Pam asked.

"I don't think this is a joke, guys," Terri said.

"Spooky is what it is," Karla said. "I'm going to assume that none of you pulled it out of that trash can." Three heads shook in response.

"I don't think this is a joke," Terri repeated. "I've had the oddest feeling in my heart ever since it landed in my french fries. Like maybe God wants us to do something with it."

Callie met Terri's gaze. "And we're just hearing about this now because...?"

Terri stirred the remains of her soda with her straw. "We had our angels, and it did seem like a great joke, totally something our husbands would pull...until now." She looked at Pam. "Will you take it?"

"Me? Why me? That thing gives me the creeps."

Terri inched it towards her dark haired friend. "We're obviously supposed to do something with it, or about it. We need more information, and you have better computer skills than the rest of us combined. You know how to navigate public information sites. Take it home, see what you can find, and let us know at Bible study Monday night."

Pam shook her head, dug her phone out of her bag, and snapped a picture of the front and back of the paper angel. "That thing is not going home with me. As far as I'm concerned we need to call Pastor Gordon to exorcise it." With the tips of two fingers she slid it back to Terri. "You keep this." She waved her phone. "I've got everything I need right here."

Terri laughed with the others as she folded the paper and tucked it into her bag. But, in the wake of her having obeyed that inner voice, she couldn't ignore the peace that settled over her heart.

~

TERRI BENT over the table to grab the edge of the wrapping paper. She jumped slightly when she felt Steve's hands on her waist. She turned, nestled into his arms, and lifted her face to accept her husband's kiss. "You got three kids into their pajamas, their teeth brushed, and a bedtime story read in less than an hour? I'm impressed."

He smiled down at her. "They were asleep by page two. You aren't the only one who had a busy day. While you melted the credit cards we went to the park and had lunch at McDonald's. While we were eating someone brought in some flyers about a live nativity scene with a petting zoo, so I took them there as well. We rode camels."

Terri inhaled deeply. "Is that what I smell?"

"Hey." Steve took a step back. "I was going to offer to help you wrap, but if you're going to insult me, I'm leaving."

"You're the most amazing man I know, a considerate husband, and a great father."

"That's better. Now, tell me what I can do."

She waved her hand at a pile of wrapped gifts. "Can you put those little ones under the tree for me? The six big boxes are for the angel kids. They need to be stacked to the side."

Terri watched him from under her lashes when she mentioned the angels, looking for any sign that he'd been privy to today's mischief. His expression gave nothing away. She looked up when he came back for the second load, still unconvinced of his innocence. "Did you talk to any of the guys today?"

"Guys?"

"Harrison, Benton, Ian..."

"No." He turned to face her, arms loaded. "Should I have?"

"I guess not." She studied him, certain that if he were in on it, she'd be able to see it. *Nothing.* "I just wondered what they did with their day...thought you might know."

"Nope, sorry." He hefted the gifts. "I'll put these under the tree, and then I need some time in my office."

"Thanks." Terri finished up the few gifts she had left. Through it all, she reflected on the mystery of Hannah's angel. It really had seemed like a practical joke until Callie opened her wallet to pay for dessert. She smiled when she remembered her friend's startled expression and Pam's promise to have the thing exorcised if it kept turning up where it shouldn't. *Weird* seemed to be the best word to describe her day.

Kids down, gifts wrapped, her husband locked away in his office, Terri finally settled on the sofa and pulled out her Bible. Tears filled her eyes as she read 1 Kings 19:11-12. "And he said, Go forth, and stand upon the mount before the Lord. And, behold, the Lord passed by, and a great and strong wind rent the mountains, and brake in pieces the rocks before the Lord; but the Lord was not in the wind: and after the wind an earthquake; but the Lord was not in the earthquake: And after the earthquake a fire; but the Lord was not in the fire: and after the fire a still small voice."

The small *keep it* she'd heard in her soul since the first appearance of the angel still echoed in her heart. Had she missed a God thing? In this season dedicated to celebrating the biggest miracle of all, why was it so hard to accept the fact that God might use a paper angel to accomplish a smaller one?

"Father, I'm sorry. I heard You and I ignored You. Help us understand what You want us to do. Guide Pam's search. Open all of our hearts to Your will in this. Because as sure as I am that You spoke to me this afternoon, I'm sure this is something You've given the four of us to accomplish together."

2

"Jeremy Alan Archer, get back in here."

Pam's eighteen-year-old son, Jeremy, stopped in his tracks and turned to face her with a sullen expression. "Mom, she's going to make me late."

"I don't care." Pam shivered in the doorway and bundled her robe around herself. "You're the reason Megan's car is in the shop. You topped off her tank with diesel. Taxi service is the least you can do while it gets repaired." She brushed a kiss against his cheek as he came back in the house. "I know you were trying to help, but—"

"Who ever said no good deed goes unpunished...?"

"Just pay more attention next time."

"Yeah, yeah." He paused at the bottom of the stairs and yelled up them. "Move your butt, Prissy Pants. I'm out of here in five, with or without you."

Seventeen-year-old Megan breezed down the stairs. "All right all ready, geesh. Let's go. I need a cappuccino."

"Not on your life."

"Mom…"

Pam closed the front door on their argument, turned the lock for good measure, and leaned against it. It would be a miracle if she survived the rest of the school year. She retreated to the home office she shared with her husband, Harrison. He was gone for the day as well, dragged out of the house earlier than normal by a meeting with a client, followed by a nine AM appearance before a judge. He'd spend the rest of his day seeing clients in the office in town. Pam figured she had about seven hours of blissful peace and quiet.

She took a deep breath and drank in the silence. There were chores to do, and Monday was her normal day to get them done, but a good mystery always came first. Pam placed a steaming cup of coffee on her desk, swiped open her phone, and brought up the picture of Hannah's angel. The breath she didn't realize she was holding expelled into the room when the picture displayed. The thing had pulled so many tricks Saturday, she'd half expected the picture to be gone. Laughter followed the exhale. *You're as goofy as a kid.* Maybe, but this thing seemed to have a life of its own.

Practical joke or the hand of God? The jury had not returned a verdict.

Pam booted up her computer and grabbed a legal pad. Under the heading *Sites to check*, she began her list. Department of human services, school records, public utilities, DMV, rental and real estate agencies, property tax registries, public police sites. The computer signaled a request for her password, and she entered it absently.

The angel made it easy to assume that Hannah was a

child, but they had all assumed it was a joke, too. *Wrong.* With nothing to go on, she went straight to Google and typed in HANNAH PRICE GARFIELD OK. If their quarry was an adult, this might be the quickest way to locate information about her. Pam felt her features settle into a frown as she paged through the search results. Hannah Price was a more common name than she'd anticipated. There were multiple matches linked to Oklahoma, but none to Garfield. She stretched her back, wiggled her fingers, and prepared to dive into cyberspace.

Two hours later, through a combination of determination, and some help from a friend with access to real estate records, Pam had her first tiny thread to tug.

A small house at 529 Oakdale Ave. had been rented by a Wesley Price three weeks ago. *Adult male instead of a female child.* Pam shrugged, wrote the address on a note card, and stuck it in her purse. It was likely a wild goose chase, but she'd do a quick drive by on her way to Bible study tonight. At least she'd have an impression to share with her friends.

～

PAM SLOWED the car to a crawl and tried to see the house numbers on Oakdale through the December gloom. Five twenty-three was illuminated by the only porch light shining on the entire block. She powered the window down and counted until she came to what she hoped was 529. A feeling of dismay filled the car as she stopped and surveyed the property. This wasn't the worst neighborhood in

Garfield, but this was certainly the worst house on the block. The small wood frame house, gray in the dusk, boasted peeling paint, a sagging porch, and windows covered with thick sheets of plastic, a pathetic screen if somebody was trying to keep winter's chill outside. A couple of the windows were boarded over, like someone just said *forget it* and gave up.

The driveway was empty, but an unsteady glow flickered through one of the house's windows. Pam frowned. It looked like candle light.

While she mulled over the condition of the house, the front door opened and a heavily pregnant woman stepped out on to the rickety porch. Other than the bulge around her middle, she was slightly built with a fall of long straight hair that looked inky black from Pam's vantage point. The woman pulled a quilt around her shoulders as she stared at Pam's car.

"Hello," Pam called through the window. "Is this 529?"

Something akin to terror lit the woman's face. She whirled, dashed back into the house, and slammed the door with a bang.

"Well, OK." Pam raised the window and put the car into gear. The mystery just got deeper.

PAM ACCEPTED the cup of coffee Callie offered and waited for Karla to return from the restroom. The Monday night Bible study had concluded, and all the guests had gone home except for the four founders of the group. They would sit for a while longer, enjoy a second piece of cheese-cake and exchange news.

While Karla dawdled, Pam picked at the remnants of her raspberry swirl cheesecake, her disposition unaccountably sour. OK, she knew what had darkened her mood, but not why. So a woman on a shabby porch had looked at her like she had the plague and refused to speak to her. Garfield was a friendly little town, but Pam worked in a law office. She knew the peaceful place held its share of lowlifes. But the look on that woman's face... *God, what are you trying to tell us?*

Snap, snap. The two quick pops next to her ear jerked Pam back to the here and now. "What?"

Callie lowered her hand. "We've been talking to you for almost two minutes. Where were you?"

Pam sipped her coffee. "At Hannah's, I think." That got their attention. Three bodies leaned forward, and three pairs of eyes locked on hers.

"You found her?" Terri asked.

Pam shook her head at the relief that flooded Terri's face. "It's too early to get excited. I found a house recently rented by a Wesley Price. All I know for sure is that there's a very pregnant woman in residence." She condensed her search into a brief explanation.

"I drove by the house on my way here tonight. It's a sad little place with a landlord who should be hung by his toenails. Other than that..." Pam lifted her shoulders. "Other than that, nothing I guess."

Terri sat back in her chair. "Well, at least we have a place to start. Whether or not it's the right house, it looks like there's a need there. What's our next move?"

Pam lifted her hands. "Beats me. We can't just show up at the door and say God sent us—"

"But—" Terri started.

"Hold up, girlfriend," Pam continued. "I'm not suggesting we ignore the situation. I'm with you in believing God wants us to do something, but I think we need a plan before we go barging into a situation we know nothing about."

Silence settled over the table as the four women sipped their coffee, each absorbed in her own thoughts.

Pam glanced at her watch and rose to take her dishes to Karla's sink. "Callie, look through your records at the clinic. See if any of your newer OB patients list that address."

Callie frowned at her. "You know I can't do that."

Pam answered the frown with one of her own and turned to Karla. "In that case, when is Nicolas due home?"

"I talked to him today," Karla said. "He and Patrick are flying back tomorrow. Kate, Sam, and the kids are staying in Florida for a few more days. Kate's parents are having a blast spoiling the kids."

Terri grinned. "Spoiling? I talked to Bobbie and Chad last night. I miss my grandbabies, but they're having so much fun on this trip. I think they've been to every amusement park Orlando has to offer...twice. My Seth and Lilly are more than jealous. They want to know when they can go to Disney World. I think we might have to make that happen sooner rather than later."

"It's a shame the guys couldn't stay longer," Pam said, "but I'm glad Nicolas is coming home. I'll give him a call later in the week. Maybe he can use some of his resources at the PD to shed some light on the residents of 529 Oakdale Ave."

～

JILLIAN TURNED in the bed and allowed Wesley to pull her close. He trailed gentle fingers over the curve of her hip and around the mound of her belly. She snuggled, never so safe or so secure as when she was in his arms.

"Go to sleep," he whispered.

"I can't, I'm worried. I don't know who that woman was or what she wanted, but what if...?"

"You can't think like that. No one is going to look for us here."

"How can you be so sure?"

Wesley turned her in his arms so he could see her face. "Your name hasn't been on a single thing we've done since we left Ohio. You said they never knew mine. As long as we keep it that way, they can look all they want, but looking is all they can do."

She closed her eyes, lay silently for a few minutes, but sleep eluded her. "How long?"

Jillian felt his shrug. He wasn't sleeping either, and he didn't need the question clarified. "The baby will be here in a month or so. If we can stay under the radar for six months, we should be in the clear. They're only interested in newborns."

"And the money I cost them." She turned her head into the side of his neck. "I'm sorry."

"Shh...babe, it's not your fault. I'm the one who freaked

out when you told me you were pregnant. If I'd stuck by you, you wouldn't have turned to those crooks for help, wouldn't have allowed them to pay your medical bills. I'm just sorry it took me so long to understand what I was walking away from. Sorry it took me so long to listen to what God was telling me."

Jillian bit her lip in the dark. "I hate living like this. Do you think God understands?"

"I have to believe He does. Marrying you..." He paused when the baby kicked under his hand. "Making a home for our child. That's all I want, but we can't risk putting your name on a public document for a while. It's too easy to trace. We're sharing a house, but we aren't..." He paused, and she knew he was searching for a gentle way to say it. "We're not fooling around anymore. He has to know that I can't leave you alone. A few months of abstinence is a small price to pay."

A small price, she thought. She hoped and prayed there would be no other cost for the wrong choices they'd made.

His voice sounded drowsy when he continued. "We won't live like this forever. I'm gonna take care of you."

Jillian put her hand over his. Wesley worked two part-time jobs. Both paid minimum-wage and the money didn't stretch very far. But they had a roof over their heads, food, and heat. Maybe after Christmas when some of the part-time workers at the local retailers thinned out, Wesley could get a real job, and they could afford to get the electricity turned on. It would be wonderful not to read by candlelight or live out of an ice chest.

She settled in for the night. *God, I know we messed up, but we've rededicated our lives to You. Please help us make this right.* Jillian fell asleep dreaming of the home she'd make for Wesley and their daughter, Hannah.

~

PAM LEFT Karla's house and detoured back to Oakdale Ave. She didn't have a name for the unrest clawing at her insides. They were doing what they could to find a solution to the mystery. These things took time, but...if the pregnant woman she'd seen was Hannah, the clock was ticking. She jerked the car to a stop. The house was completely dark now, but there was a car in the driveway that hadn't been there earlier. Excitement surged as Pam inched forward, hoping to shed just enough light from her headlights to copy down a tag number. That information would go a long way once Nicolas started digging.

Anticipation crashed into the rocky shores of disappointment. The car was parked nose to the street, so there was no plate visible from the road. *Luck or design?* Pam leaned toward believing the latter as she continued her drive home.

She opened the front door as an explosion rocked the living room. The noise of the video game died away, quickly replaced by Megan's hoots of triumph.

"Take that, Dork Face."

Jeremy's response was a growl. "Blind luck, Prissy Pants. Two out of three."

Pam grinned at the all-purpose nicknames her children still used for each other. At least the tone tonight was friendly instead of the lines-drawn-in-the-sand, full out war that seemed the norm, even though her children were nearly adults. But the noise had to go. She hurried forward, interrupting Megan's vigorous victory dance.

"Guys, you need to call a Christmas truce on that thing. Peace on earth and all that."

"Oh, Mom, one more game." Megan pleaded. "This is the first time I've had him where I want him since he bought the stupid thing."

"I didn't tell you to turn it off, just down," she clarified. "Where's Harrison?"

"Upstairs hiding under his headphones, working on briefs for next week," Jeremy answered. "We'll turn it down."

"Thank you, but just one more game. Everyone has work or school tomorrow."

Her daughter came around the couch and placed a kiss on her cheek. "Thanks, Mom." She faced Jeremy. "Saddle up, Dork Face. You're a dead man walking." A throw pillow sailed over Pam's head, and hit Megan square in the face.

How quickly things could go from calm to confrontational with these two. Pam stepped toward the stairs. "Guys, truce, OK? And Megan, I'll know it if you throw that pillow back at your brother." She left the room but paused on the first step, listening to her kids, taking in the blessings of her family and home. Warmth, light...bickering. Things she took for granted every day. *Father, I'm so blessed.* The words of silent praise settled the weight of the mystery a little heavier on her shoulders. *Please show us what we're missing.*

3

N ewton Stark pushed into his assistant's office Wednesday morning without knocking. "Have you found that girl yet?"

Fletcher looked up and shook his head. "Not yet, Mr. Stark."

Newton leaned his ample girth across the desk, one fist pounded on the wood to emphasize his words. "That baby is due any day. There's a hundred thousand dollars on the line here. Your continued incompetence is unacceptable."

"We're looking." Fletcher cringed when his voice squeaked. We've hired detectives under the ruse of finding your missing daughter. They've faxed her picture to every OB clinic within a five-state radius, asking for information, offering a reward. It's like she fell off the face of the earth."

"Bah!" Newton spun on a heel and left the room. *Fell off the face of the earth.* The slam of the door echoed and had the resident paralegals seated at their desks looking up in surprise. He forced a smile, waved them back to their paperwork, and continued to his own office. He and Fletcher were the only people in the office aware of their firm's little sideline. He intended to keep it that way.

Safe in his office, the smile changed to a frown. That girl owed him, and when he got his hands on her, he'd take the baby and extract every penny he'd expended on chasing her out of her skinny hide. He threw himself into his desk chair and looked at the photo of the smiling couple he'd handpicked from his private files. Not only would they make good parents, but they were wealthy enough, and desperate enough, to pay his fee.

He shook his head. It wasn't as if he stole the babies he placed. He had a contract with each of their mothers. He paid for their medical and living expenses while they were pregnant, and once they were delivered of their unwanted bundles of joy, he got the baby, and Mom went back to her unencumbered life, no worse, or wiser, for the wear. Once he matched the babies to a couple from his file, it was a win-win situation. The girls got the best care available, the adoptive couple got a baby, and he got a nice fat fee. It worked, until it didn't.

Newton laid the picture back on the desk. At least he hadn't contacted the perspective parents yet. The service he provided wasn't strictly legal, but the babies he placed were better off with their adoptive parents than they would be with some dimwitted girl who couldn't be bothered to swallow a birth control pill once a day.

Dimwitted? He frowned. Jillian Rishi had outwitted him so far, but the game wasn't over yet.

～

TERRI AND PAM sat in the car in front of 529 Oakdale Ave. Terri huffed out a breath and watched it billow from her mouth in a dense fog. Pam had the heater running full out, and she was still freezing.

"No electricity...you're sure about that?"

"As positive as I can be without personally trying the light switches," Pam answered. "I talked to a friend at the utilities department. The water and gas were turned on three weeks ago under the name Wesley Price, but not the power. Add in the fact that both times I've been by here, the place has been completely dark except for what looked like candle light..."

You need to go inside.

Heavenly direction or Terri snoopiness? She studied the house, her lower lip caught between her teeth. "The bottoms scheduled to drop out of our temperatures tonight. Single digits for the next few days."

"Probably why the gas is on and the electricity isn't. I'll bet there's no central heat and air." She pointed. "See that small window air conditioner unit? A lot of these old houses have standalone gas heaters in the main rooms."

Who should have to make a choice between heat or light? Terri reached for the door handle. She was going in. "You coming?"

"Right behind you," Pam said, "but I wish, just once, God would fill us in on His plan *before* we got knee deep into the problem."

Wouldn't that be nice? Terri kept the thought to herself as they approached the door. Loose boards groaned in protest as she stepped onto the porch. She waited until Pam stood beside her before opening the tattered screen and knocking. They looked at each other when the door slipped open under Terri's first rap.

"What do we do now?"

"Announce ourselves, I guess," Pam answered, her voice low and hesitant.

"Hello?" Terri took a single step across the threshold and halted when her foot landed on something that emitted a loud squeak. Startled by the unexpected noise, she lowered her eyes to the floor and searched for the source. The light streaming in through the open door illuminated a dark form crouched at her feet. A barely restrained shriek clawed its way up her throat as reflex kicked in. She jumped back, taking Pam with her

"What are you doing?"

Terri's heart pounded double time as she peeked back inside, her eyes locked on the offensive little beast.

"Mouse."

Pam huffed and shoved her aside. When the offensive beast didn't scamper away, she nudged it with the toe of her shoe and bent down for a closer look. "Wimp. It's a mouse all right. The rubber, cat-toy type."

Terri peered over her friend's shoulder. "You sure?"

Pam nudged it a second time. It squeaked at her but offered no further threat.

Nerves restored, Terri pushed the door wider and surveyed her surroundings while her heartbeat and breathing returned to normal. The curtains were drawn, casting the room in shadows except for the bright sliver of light from the open front door. The floors were worn hardwood and bore the marks of decades of traffic. The colorful throw rugs scattered here and there put her in mind of a wrinkled old granny in a new spring dress.

Terri took a breath, preparing to call out again, and paused. She cocked her head. "Did you hear that?"

"Another mouse?" Pam asked, her voice just a little too sweet.

"Haha. No, listen."

"Please help me."

Terri and Pam glanced at each other, then moved as one down the shadowy hall. The door at the end was open, the room empty except for a mattress lying on the floor in one corner of the room. The opposite corner held an old-fashioned gas space heater. Even though the grates burned a cherry red the room was still chilly.

Movement from the bed drew Terri's attention. A slight figure buried beneath a mound of blankets shifted. The motion displaced a large gray cat. Terri watched as the animal slid to the floor, arched its back in a feline stretch, then sat and began to groom itself.

Terri moved closer to the mattress. "Hannah?"

"No…Jillian." The woman turned to lie on her back, the blankets accenting the mound of a late term pregnancy. Long black hair lay in a tousled, dark mess on the pillow, her eyes remained shut. Terri tilted her head and looked closer. The young woman's eyes weren't just closed. They were squeezed shut against pain.

Terri's gaze slid to the Jillian's belly. "Are you in labor? Do you need an ambulance?"

"No!" The word rang loudly in the room, and Jillian's hands came out from under the covers. They shook as she brought them to her temples. "No doctors. It's not the baby.

I have a headache." Tears seeped from under the clamped eyelids. "It hurts so bad. I can't see, I can't think..."

Terri went to her knees on the edge of the mattress. "You poor thing. I had a couple of migraines like that when I was pregnant." She looked at Pam. "Go find the bathroom and bring her a cold washcloth." After Pam left, Terri brushed hair from Jillian's face and laid a hand on her forehead. "Anything else going on? Fever, nausea?" Her hand moved to rest on Jillian's stomach. "Cramps?"

Pam came back with the wet cloth and a glass of water in one hand, two white tablets in the other. "I found some Tylenol in the bathroom." She knelt on the other side of the mattress. "Can you sit up?"

Pam and Terri crouched to either side of her and helped her raise herself up long enough to swallow the pills. She lay back down, and Pam placed the cold compress on her forehead.

Some of the tension left Jillian's face. "Thank you," she whispered.

"What about those other things?" Terri asked again.

"No, just the headache."

Terri sighed in relief. "That's good news. How far along are you?"

A slight smile tugged at the corners of Jillian's mouth. "Eight months. Hannah will be a Christmas baby."

～

TERRI PUT a finger to her lips when she opened the door of the rundown house for Callie and Karla.

"How is she?" Callie whispered.

"Napping," Terri said. "The acetaminophen probably took the edge off, but I can say from experience, if her migraines are like mine, sleep is the best cure."

Karla took a seat in one of the two lawn chairs that furnished the living room. "I can't believe we found her."

"Not even a her...technically," Pam said. "Not for four more weeks anyway." She looked around the bare room and shivered. The temperature was dropping, and the single gas heater wasn't keeping up. "And now that we've found her, what are we supposed to do?"

Callie pressed her lips together and looked at Terri. "You said her name was Jillian?"

Terri nodded.

Callie opened her purse and withdrew a folded piece of paper. She shook it open, focused on it for a second, and held it out.

Terri took the paper, read it, and passed it to Pam. "That's her."

Karla held out a hand and Pam gave her the paper. "Missing," Karla read aloud. "Jillian Stark. Reward for any information leading to the safe return of our daughter." She looked up. "Where did you get this?"

"It came over the office fax a couple of weeks ago." Callie said. She retrieved the paper and held it up to the stingy winter light filtering through the plastic-coated windows. The image on the flyer was of a twentyish year old woman of Indian descent with long black hair. "Terri's description matched this, so I brought it along." She flicked the bottom of the paper. "The number at the bottom connects to a law office in Ohio." She looked at Terri. "I called it."

"Callie!"

"Relax. I hung up without talking to anyone. I just figured we needed to know as much as we could about who and what we're dealing with."

~

JILLIAN'S EYES FLUTTERED OPEN. The headache still pounded, but it was better. At least she could focus her eyes now. Not being able to see clearly was almost the scariest thing she'd ever experienced. She lifted her head, and a small groan filled the room. The muscles in her neck were sore, and the skin on her scalp felt too tight, like her skull had grown an inch all around.

As she looked up at the ceiling, a strange sensation nagged at her, like she was forgetting something important. Wait...had there been...? She held her breath and listened. Sure enough, voices filtered in from down the hall. Her glance went to the window. Still too light for Wesley to be home. Jillian's heart pounded beneath her breastbone, and fear drove the pain in her head back to a nearly unbearable level. *Have they found me?* She needed to get away, she needed to find Wesley. She needed to pee.

Jillian struggled to sit up. Shadow sat in the tangled covers blinking at her. The cat's calm presence reassured her a little. She held out her hand, and the cat moved in for a rub. "I'll feed you in a second, but I need the bathroom first. She rolled to the edge of the mattress, reached for the windowsill, and used it to pull herself up. The bigger Hannah got, the harder it was for Jillian to get up and down.

Once she had her feet under her, she crept to the door and listened. The voices were female, which eased her mind a bit. He wouldn't send women after her...maybe. The bathroom door stood ajar and inviting across the hall. She needed to know who was in the living room, but she couldn't face anything with a bladder that hadn't been emptied since early this morning. Jillian peeked out, didn't see anyone, and dashed into the tiny room. The voices from the other room stopped.

They know I'm awake.

Jillian used the restroom and took the time to brush her teeth and run a brush through her hair. She still felt like crap, but the simple acts of hygiene boosted her confidence. Her long flannel nightgown brushed her sock-covered feet and was hardly suitable for company, but she figured taking the time to change clothes was pushing her luck.

She stepped into the living room doorway and gasped. Four women looked her way, not just the two she vaguely remembered. Jillian crossed her arms. "What are you people doing in my house?"

A slender woman with a short shaggy haircut and a pleasant smile took a step forward. "Are you feeling better?"

The voice triggered the memory of cool fingers on her forehead, the soothing touch of a cold cloth that followed.

The wariness of waking up with strangers in her house receded a bit. If they meant her harm, they'd had ample opportunity to do whatever they wanted. "Thank you for your help earlier. That was the worst headache I've ever had. I appreciate what you did, but you haven't answered my question."

The woman smiled, came to Jillian's side, wrapped an arm around her shoulders, and guided her to one of the chairs. "We do need to talk, but you need to sit. I can still see pain in your eyes." She looked at her watch. "It's been about three hours since your last dose of Tylenol." She stopped and looked at one of the other women. This one had long, nearly black hair. "Pam, can you get her a couple more pills?"

Pam hurried from the room. Jillian recognized her from earlier as well.

The shaggy haired brunette held out a hand. "I'm Terri Evans."

Before Jillian had time to react to the introduction, Shadow glided into the room and jumped into her lap. He looked at her and emitted a pitiful meow. Jillian nudged him to the floor and pushed herself out of the chair. "He wants his breakfast."

"I'll take care of it." A woman with short blond hair motioned toward the kitchen. "In there?"

Jillian nodded and sank back down. "Under the sink."

Pam came back and handed Jillian a couple of pills and a glass of water. The woman laid a hand on her chest. "I'm Pam Lake." While Jillian swallowed the pills, Pam motioned to a woman with silver hair. "This is Karla McAlister. Callie Stillman is feeding your cat.

The blonde came back from the kitchen. "All done."

Jillian watched as the four women looked at each other. None of them looked threatening, but not a single one had offered to answer her question. She bent forward and placed the glass on the floor. Wesley would be here soon. He would not take their presence lightly, especially if she couldn't explain.

"It's a pleasure to meet all of you, but I'm sure you can understand my need of some sort of explanation."

Terri dragged the remaining chair over, took a seat right in front of Jillian, and studied her closely. "Your name is Jillian Stark?"

"Jillian Rishi," she corrected, but her heart sped up at the incorrect last name. *Just be still. Don't volunteer any information. Let them explain.*

Terri sent a look to Callie, then placed a hand on Jillian's belly. "This is Hannah?"

"How did you...?"

"You mentioned the baby's name right before you went to sleep." Terri stopped, glanced at her friends, and received three quick nods. She reached into her purse and brought out a folded piece of paper. "We think God told us to come help you and Hannah."

Jillian sat back in her chair. "What?"

Terri straightened the paper out on her knee and handed it to Jillian. "It all started with this stubborn paper angel."

4
_____

By the time Terri finished her story, Jillian didn't know whether to laugh or cry. She fingered the faded ketchup stain on one of the angel's wings. Had God orchestrated this comedy in answer to her daily pleas for His help?

Terri touched her knee, and Jillian looked up. "All of the pieces of our part of the story fit, outlandish though they may be. We're—"

"All but one." Callie took a step forward and turned the paper angel over. "You said your last name is Rishi, but the writing here says Price." She shook out a second piece of paper and held it out. "This says Stark."

Jillian took the paper. She frowned at her own picture before reading the text. She went lightheaded. The back of her neck scalded with a sticky heat, her hands began to shake, and she couldn't catch her breath. Sounds receded, she'd never fainted in her life but... *They'd found her.*

Terri forced Jillian's head down as far as Hannah's bulk

would allow. Someone else chafed her hands to warm them. She heard the voices from a distance, unable to identify who said what.

"What just happened?"

"Jillian, are you OK?"

"Someone get a fresh glass of water. Jillian, take some slow deep breaths."

Broken sobs racked Jillian's chest, but the words penetrated, and she complied with the instructions. After her breathing came under control, she sat up and accepted the glass of water Pam placed into her hands.

Terri leaned forward, her expression intense. "Look at me." She gathered Jillian's hands in hers. "Long slow breaths."

"But—"

"We'll get to the buts. For now, I want you to focus on me and breathe. No one here is going to hurt you."

Oh, how Jillian wanted to believe them.

The front door slammed open. "What's going on in here?" Wesley shoved through the knot of women and knelt by Jillian's side. "Baby, look at me. Are you OK?"

Jillian managed a nod.

"I think she's fine," Terri said. "She had a bit of a panic attack is all."

Wesley sat back on his heels, his glare moving from one woman to another before settling back on Jillian.

"Jillian?"

"I'm good." She took a final deep breath. She pointed out each woman in turn. "Wesley, this is Terri, Pam, Callie, and Karla." She nodded at Wesley. "This is Wesley Price, Hannah's father."

Callie put a finger to her lip. "With everything that's happened, I'd forgotten the name on the rental."

Jillian closed her eyes. These women had done some serious connecting the dots to get from a paper angel to the living room of this shabby little house. She had to believe there was some divine intervention going on. *Haven't I been praying for just that?*

She tugged Wesley's hand until she had his full attention. Jillian looked into his hazel eyes. She saw fierce protectiveness coupled with uncertainty. After all they'd been through, she appreciated the first and identified with the second. "You know how we've been praying for help?" When he nodded she continued, "Let me tell you an amazing story."

Jillian handed him the tattered paper angel and told Wesley about her day. She started with the debilitating headache and the women who'd miraculously come to her aide. Next she related the tale of the angel who refused to stay tied to the tree. Each appearance she shared brought a bigger smile to Wesley's face. She finished with the flyer that had given her such a start.

She handed it to him, and his smile disappeared. "I knew they'd look for you, but this is more than I expected." He crumpled the paper and tossed it away. "Go get dressed. We'll leave tonight. I won't let them find you."

Wesley started to move from his position by Jillian's knees, but Callie put a hand on his shoulder. "I don't think that's a good idea."

Wesley climbed to his feet. "Look, I appreciate what you did this afternoon, but it's my job to keep Jillian and Hannah safe. This is really none of your business—"

"I don't know, Wesley." Terri moved to stand next to Callie. "Seems like God's gone to some pretty extreme measures over the last few days to make it our business."

Pam stepped to his side and rubbed a hand up and down his arm. "I know you're feeling a little ambushed. I'm sorry for that, but we'd like to help if you'll let us."

Jillian watched Wesley run a hand through his hair. The action told her he was wrestling with himself.

"Wesley," she said, feeling stronger and more certain by the second, "I know it's hard to trust anyone right now, but we've been praying for help." He turned to look at her, and she rubbed a hand over her stomach and met his eyes. "I don't think running is a good idea if we can avoid it. The Bible says to pray expecting an answer, but what good does the answer do if we don't accept it when it comes?"

Wesley put his hands on his hips and studied the floor. "How can they help?" he muttered.

"Well, for starters," Karla said, "I can get you out of this hovel and into a trailer with power and furniture."

"The RV," Terri said. "What a great idea."

Karla shrugged. "It's sitting empty, so we might as well put it to use."

Callie pulled out her phone. "Say the word, and I'll have my husband hook up his truck and drag it out of the storage lot. You two can sleep in a real bed tonight." She shivered. "And you won't have to worry about the cold front that's on its way."

"You'll be snug as two bugs in a rug," Karla agreed. The cat twisted around her feet. "Well, too bugs and a nosy feline."

Jillian closed her eyes. After three weeks on a mattress

in the floor, the bed alone was enough to sell her on the idea. "What do you say, Wesley? Do we tell them the whole story and accept their help, or pack up the car? I love you, and I trust you. I'll do whichever you think is best."

Wesley exhaled and focused on the women. His gaze settled on the one with the short haircut. Terri, and he spoke. "There are some things you need to know before you get too involved."

Terri rubbed her hands together, taking his words as progress. "Jillian go get dressed. If we're going to talk, let's do it some place warm, over dinner, my treat."

THE WINTER SUN was setting in the west in a blaze of orange when Terri pulled open the door to Lizzie's Diner. Toward the north, the clouds hung gray and heavy with the promised arctic cold front. The very thought made her shiver. She shepherded Wesley and Jillian in ahead of her and steered them to the eight-seat table along the back wall. The diner was fairly empty. Most of the churches in town had service tonight. That and the promised change in the weather should give them some quiet and privacy for their discussion.

The four women scooted into the seats against the wall. Terri didn't know what had the young couple so spooked, but she wanted to be able to see who came and went and who, if anyone, might be overly interested in their conversation. Jillian and Wesley took the middle two chairs on the other side with their backs to the room.

"Have you been here?" Terri asked.

Wesley and Jillian shook their heads. "We've been trying to keep a low profile," Jillian answered.

"That, and my little paycheck doesn't afford many meals out," Wesley added.

"Got'cha." Terri plucked menus from the middle of the table and passed them across. "They serve a great breakfast any time of the day, and"—she sniffed the air, reveling in the smell of hot burgers and fries—"they make the best hamburgers in town. Order whatever you want."

A young waitress approached their table. "Hey, Grandma."

Callie smiled. "Hi, April, I thought this was your night off."

"Supposed to be, but one of the other girls called in sick. I'm filling in. What can I get everyone to drink?" She noted their responses and hurried away, leaving the six people at the table to peruse the menus. April returned in a matter of minutes, delivered their drinks, and departed a short time later with their dinner requests.

Terri watched the girl push through the swinging doors of the kitchen before she leaned forward. For whatever reason, her three friends had ceded the lead in this project to her, and she was anxious to get some answers. "We've probably got thirty minutes before our dinner comes out," she told Jillian and Wesley. "You know our side of the story and the events that led us to your door. Are you going to let us help you?"

Jillian and Wesley shared a look and clasped their hands on the table. Jillian picked up her glass of tea with her free hand and sucked a deep drink through the straw.

She set the glass down, taking time to align it in a circle of moisture on the table.

"Wesley and I came here from Ohio three weeks ago."

Callie stirred sweetener into her tea. "That's quite a trip given your advanced pregnancy. Where in Ohio?"

"A little town outside Ottawa Hills, close to the Michigan border." Jillian bit her lip. "Probably not anyplace you'd recognize."

"Yeah," Wesley said. "Just this little middle-of-no-place...place." He looked at Jillian. "We grew up there. My dad pastors one of the local Pentecostal congregations."

"And mine is the priest at a Hindu Temple," Jillian said.

Terri raised her eyebrows. "Talk about star-crossed lovers."

"Romeo and Juliet, Samson and Delilah, Sir Lancelot and Guinevere...Wesley and Jillian." Jillian stopped and smiled when Wesley raised her hand and brushed a kiss across her knuckles.

"Couples who had no business together," he said.

"But we fell in love." She straightened in her seat and met the gazes across the table. "My family is third generation American, but they've clung to the traditional religion. It is the tradition in our family that the children of a Hindu priest are expected to follow in the father's footsteps. As the only child in the family, and since the stance against female priests is changing, I've been groomed since I could talk to take my place as priest after my father." She frowned. "Do you know that there are hundreds of gods worshiped in the Hindu religion? Benevolent, angry, monstrous...creatures. I never understood the mindless ritual of it all. Never felt any fulfillment in worshiping something with eight limbs and snakes for hair." Jillian shook her head.

"When I met Wesley and started sneaking out to visit his church. I found out that I could have a personal relationship with the one true God." She laid a hand over her heart. "It made so much more sense, and once I asked Christ into my life, it brought such peace. I knew what I wanted for myself." Her breath shuddered heavy in her lungs. "My father was furious."

"And mine wasn't much better," Wesley said. "He was thrilled that Jillian had accepted Christ, but a Hindu priest as a prospective in-law? That wasn't going to happen."

"The feeling was very mutual," Jillian agreed. "Our parents weren't even going to pretend to get along."

Wesley took a deep breath, his smile sheepish. "But we always got along just fine."

Jillian closed her eyes. "We got along a little too fine graduation night." Silence greeted her blunt comment.

"And Hannah is the product of that?" Pam asked.

Jillian nodded and gave a half shrug. "We planned to get married after we finished college. But...things got a little carried away and...we...we messed up."

"When Jillian told me about the baby, I freaked out." Wesley ran his hands through his hair. "I was going to be a father? My world just dropped out from under me. We were eighteen and barely out of high school. This news was going to cause major upheaval for both families."

He lowered his eyes, and Terri saw the red that crept up from beneath his collar.

When he continued, his voice was a whisper. "I ran." He looked up, and there was moisture in his eyes. "My older brother is stationed in Germany. Mom and Dad offered to send me for a six-month visit as a graduation present. I told them no at first. I figured they were trying to separate us, but when Jillian..." He swallowed. "I didn't know what to do. I told my parents we'd broken it off and accepted their offer."

Wesley leaned his head against Jillian's. "I'm so sorry."

Jillian turned and brushed a kiss across his temple. "You came back. That's what matters."

Terri swallowed back emotion and addressed her next question to Jillian. "What did you do after he left?"

"I got out of town too. My parents would have pushed for an abortion. That wasn't an option, but neither was raising a child on my own with no family support. A friend of a friend of a friend knew about a lawyer in Columbus who does private adoptions. I should have known something wasn't right when he insisted I come to his office after hours, but he gave me this nice little speech about the good he was doing. He'd put me up in an apartment, pay for my medical expenses, and find a family to love my baby." She hung her head. "Giving the baby up was breaking my heart, but I was coping until Wesley emailed me and said that God hadn't let him rest since he got on the plane to Germany. He said if I'd have him, he was ready to face what we'd done. He wanted to marry me, make a home for our daughter." Jillian wiped a tear from her eye.

"That was the longest five months of my life," Wesley said. "Every time I closed my eyes it was like God had a picture of Jillian's face painted on the inside of my eyelids or something. I finally broke down and confessed the whole thing to my brother. He took me to see the pastor of their church. Once I rededicated my life, I couldn't get back here fast enough."

Jillian picked up the story. "Mr. Stark had been kind to me. I didn't feel right about just leaving, so we went to his office to tell him that I'd changed my mind."

"I had some savings," Wesley added. "I wanted to pay him back for what he'd spent. He laughed at us."

"But we stood our ground..." Her voice dropped to a whisper. "The man went ballistic, yelling and swiping folders off his desk. I don't know what would have happened if his phone hadn't rung. He wasn't any happier with the call than he was with us, because his face got redder the longer he listened. He told us to wait for him and stormed out of his office."

"We were so stunned, we didn't know what to do," Wesley said. "I started gathering up some of the paperwork. Pictures of babies and couples...contracts..."

Jillian swiped at her face. "That's when we found out that the adoption thing was a scam. Our baby would get adopted all right, but she'd go to whichever family could pay the highest price. They weren't just placing babies for adoption, they were selling them."

"We left his office, got in the car, and started driving," Wesley said.

Jillian grabbed napkins from the dispenser in the center of the table and mopped her face. "And now they're looking for me, and if they find us, they'll drag me back to Ohio and take our baby away from us." She looked at the women across the table. "Please tell us that you have a way to keep that from happening."

Wesley gathered Jillian close as she gave into tears.

"We've really messed this up. We can't even get married. If we put her name on a public document, they might find us. We can't get medical help for the same reason. Even if we could afford a doctor"—he looked at Callie—"it looks like they have the clinics on alert. He rubbed Jillian's back and lowered his head to hers.

"The flyers were a long shot." Callie said. "But the reward might have been effective there, to the right person."

Terri sat back. *Messed up* didn't begin to cover what this was. She looked around the sparsely populated diner. No one seemed to be paying any attention to the drama at their table. "Wow." She leaned forward to see three other expressions of disbelief on the faces of her friends.

Jillian mopped her face with a napkin. "Can you help us?"

Terri wanted to offer a bucketful of promises, but all that came out was, "I don't know."

April returned with dinner plates, and while she distributed food, Terri mulled Jillian's question and possible answers.

"Everyone got what they need?" April asked. With answering nods all around, she smiled. "Leave room for dessert. Lizzie made pecan pie, and with the storm moving in, we have plenty."

Once she scooted away, Terri held out her hands and bowed her head. When the rest of the group had joined hands, she prayed. "Father, thank You for Your provision. And thank You for allowing us to find Jillian and Wesley in good time. We need..." She paused, unsure what to ask for. She felt Pam squeeze her hand on one side, and Callie on the other. The unity bolstered her. "We need wisdom, Father."

Terri took a deep breath and stabbed a bite of her taco salad. "Thoughts, ladies?"

Karla cut a piece of her chicken fried steak and looked over her fork. "I still think the issue of better housing is our first concern."

"But where can we put it?" Pam asked. "Wesley's right. Callie saw the flyer at work, who knows what other businesses they targeted." She looked around the diner. "After hearing their story, I'm not even sure coming here was a good idea, and I know every soul in the place. We have to get Jillian away from everyone."

Karla sprinkled pepper over the top of her gravy. "I've got some ideas about that. Do you guys remember a few years ago when Mitch took that delinquent youngster under his wing? We became friends with the boy's grandparents. They have several acres outside of town with a huge pond right in the middle of the property. It's a great camping place, and they've had it set up with water and electric hookups to accommodate a couple of campers. I bet they'd let us put the RV out there with very little explanation."

Karla turned to face Jillian. "You'd have all the comforts of home, and you wouldn't be confined to the trailer. Once this cold snap is over, you could get out, exercise and explore."

Karla sat back, and Terri grinned at the pleased look on her friend's face. She leaned forward on an elbow. "You guys game? We can get you settled in tonight and tackle some of the other problems over the next few days."

Pam spoke up. "My husband is a lawyer. He's going to want in on this."

"So will Nicolas." Karla focused on Wesley. "That's my son. He's a detective here in town. You can trust him to do what needs to be done."

Wesley and Jillian looked at each other, indecision on both faces.

"Cops and lawyers?" Wesley asked. "I'm not sure I like the sound of that."

"Let's get you settled in the RV for now. You two can talk it over, sleep on it." Callie sat back. "One more thing we can deal with short term. I work for the best OB doc in the area. He's retiring after the first of the year, but I bet he could squeeze in one more Christmas baby."

Jillian tried to stifle a sob with her hand and failed. She turned to Wesley and melted into his arms.

5

J illian cracked her eyes open the next morning. The gray winter light filtering through the windows made it hard to know just how early, or late, it was. A harsh blast of wind rattled the windows of the RV. It sounded cold, and she snuggled back under the covers. *Let it blow*. For the first time in weeks, worries about what the day might bring took a backseat. God was on His throne, she and Wesley were together, Shadow purred at her side, and four unexpected angels had their backs.

The mattress dipped beside her, and the aroma of coffee teased her eyes fully open. Wesley smiled down at her, a steaming mug held in each hand. Giving up on the notion of continued sleep, she levered herself up in the bed, struggling to situate the pillows behind her as best she could. Nothing physical was easy these days. Jillian couldn't wait to meet her daughter, but she looked forward to getting her body back almost as much.

Her thrashing woke the cat. He gave her a disdainful

look, jumped from the bed, and disappeared with a twitch of his tail. Jillian settled into the nest of pillows, and Wesley handed her one of the mugs.

"Here you go, complete with chocolate creamer."

"Really?"

"Yeah, the groceries they hauled in here have us pretty well stocked for the foreseeable future."

Jillian took a cautious taste. The sweet, rich brew slid down her throat like silk and elicited a grateful sigh. "Oh, that's amazing." She swallowed a second drink. "You and chocolate, my two favorite things to wake up to."

She released a contented sigh. "It's like a miracle, isn't it? I was almost afraid to open my eyes this morning. Yesterday seemed like a fantasy, and I wanted to keep living it."

"Yeah, well..." Wesley took a deep drink from his own mug. "Are you feeling better today?" The question held a tone she couldn't identify.

"Much." Jillian studied Wesley's unshaved face. There was something off in his expression as well as his voice. The black stubble made him look rakish and just a little dangerous. The small gold hoop earring he'd acquired in Germany reminded her of the hero in a pirate movie. She tilted her head, her eyes searching his.

"What's wrong?"

"What could possibly be wrong?" He lifted his mug and swept it in an arc in front of him. "Snug as a bug, just as advertised." He lowered the mug and frowned into its depths. "No thanks to me."

The words were muttered so softly, Jillian almost missed them. Almost. He'd worked so hard. The evidence of his wounded pride tore at her heart. She slid her hand across the soft comforter and clasped Wesley's free hand in hers. "Oh, Wesley, that's not true. It's been a path, don't you see? You came back for me when I'd almost given up hope. You rescued me and Hannah, you worked to provide for us and keep us safe, and you were brave enough, man enough, to admit we needed help. That makes you my hero, from the top of your cowlick all the way down to the frayed laces of your Nikes."

She tugged on his hand until he looked up. When he met her eyes, she continued, "It might be a little hard to see from where you're sitting, but my eyes are wide open. I love you." She started when a small foot kicked hard enough to rustle the blanket. "We love you."

Wesley lifted their clasped hands to his mouth and kissed her fingers. "I love you both so much it scares me." He let go of her and stood up. "Ignore me. I don't mean to sound ungrateful, I'm just...uneasy about some of the things our new friends said last night."

"The cops and lawyers part?"

"Yeah." He moved to the suitcase lying open on a counter under a window and shook out a clean shirt. "If it was just me, I'd go to the cops in a heartbeat, but..." His hand ran through his hair. "How do we know who we can trust? There's too much at stake to risk a wrong decision. Can't we just accept the generosity of our new friends and let it go at that?"

Jillian watched him get ready for work. "I've been thinking about that. I think this goes way beyond us." She set her mug aside, then rested her hands on her belly and the baby nestled inside. "I know that God is going to keep us safe. I know that He sent help when we needed it the most, but...what about the next woman?"

He raised an eyebrow at her.

She circled her hands on the taut skin that concealed their child...her heart. "Wesley, these people prey on women who're scared and think they have no options. If we can help put a stop to that, don't you think we should?"

Wesley's gaze went to the floor.

"I think this is the next step on that whole path thing," she said. "What if all of this has all been for a higher purpose?" Jillian paused and struggled for words to express the conclusion she'd reached while she'd slept. "I don't think it was God's will that we made Hannah before we got married, but once we made that choice, maybe He thought He could use it to help someone...lots of someones." She bit her lip and met his eyes. "I don't think I can take my baby and run away to spend my life with you, knowing that I turned my back on the chance to help someone else achieve the same thing."

"Are you sure we can trust them?"

"I think we have to start somewhere, and this feels like the right thing to do."

He tucked in his shirt. "My head knows you're right, but my heart isn't ready to agree—"

"Wesley—"

"No." He motioned to the cheap cell phone Karla had left on the nightstand. "Call them. Tell them we'll talk to the cop and the lawyer." He took the three steps to the bedside and leaned down to kiss her. He tucked a long strand of black hair behind her ear before he straightened and held out his little finger. "You've got me right here,

Jillian Rishi. You know that, right? What am I going to do when there are two of you?"

"Run for the hills?"

He shook his head. "Not ever again."

～

THURSDAY MORNING only darkened Newton Stark's mood. He stared at Jillian's picture. Her smooth mocha skin, silky black hair, and large doe-shaped eyes had captured his interest from the beginning. He didn't deal in mixed race babies very often, but he'd recently acquired a couple of clients of Eastern Indian descent. Incredibly wealthy clients. This infant could have brought him one of the highest prices he'd ever dared ask. He slammed his fist onto the desk.

"Blasted, ungrateful girl!" His head jerked up at a knock on his door. "What?"

The door cracked open, and his secretary peeked inside. "You have a call on your private line, Mr. Stark. It's been holding for several minutes."

He glanced down at the phone. *Did it ring?* "I've got it," he snapped. "Get back to work." He snatched the phone up. "Stark here."

"Good morning, Mr. Stark. Just wanted to let you know that Mary Tippons delivered a handsome baby boy last night. We've moved her off the maternity floor and isolated the boy per your standing instructions. When can we expect you?"

Newton ran a hand across his mouth when he recognized Nurse Beverly's voice. *Finally, some good news.* All his baby mothers delivered at the Regional Women's Center. The facility was older and a bit outdated when compared to the newer birthing centers in the large hospitals, but it was private and suited his needs perfectly. With the help of the doctor and the two nurses on his payroll, he controlled every aspect of the new mother's environment. She would be allowed no visitors, she would see no other staff, and most importantly, she would not see the baby.

"Wonderful. Any problems I should know about?"

"None," Beverly said. "Textbook delivery, mother and baby both doing well. The boy is seven pounds, four ounces, and nineteen inches long. I'll text you a picture."

"You do that. I'll be in right after lunch with the final paperwork. The standard deposit will be made to your account just as soon as the deal is finalized."

"Thank you, Mr. Stark. I'll be watching for you."

Newton cradled the receiver and picked up his cell phone just as it buzzed with an incoming text. The baby pictured on his screen slept peacefully, waiting to meet the people he'd spend his life with. *Let's see what we can find.*

Newton rose and locked his door. He shoved the credenza aside, opened the door to the hidden space below, and fingered through a few folders. He withdrew one and carried it back to his desk. The first item in the file was a picture of a thirty-something couple, both blond, both wearing eager smiles, both employed in lucrative careers. He placed the cell phone with the infant's picture next to them and studied the match.

A perfect little family stared back at him. This is what

he did. He made families. Yes, the money was good, not going to deny that, but... He looked back at the pictures, pleased with himself, certain that the positive he did outweighed the negative. This child would have a privileged life, thanks to him. Mary Tippons could get back to doing whatever she did. And who knew? Maybe she'd contact him again if she found herself in trouble a second time. He'd had more than one repeat client. He tapped the picture of the couple. Most importantly, these two would get the baby they wanted so desperately.

This was the exciting part. The call that put it all in motion. A call he never made until the merchandise was delivered. He wanted no disappointed couples in his office. A mom in tears and an angry father demanding answers while Stark handed back a large check...the very thought made him shudder. He found a phone number in the file, punched it into his cell phone. And did a mental hand rub as it rang.

"Hello."

"Mrs. Burns?"

"Yes."

"Newton Stark here." He smiled at the sharp indrawn breath on the other end of the connection."

"Mr. Stark, do you...do you have something for us?"

"Indeed. Can you hold for just a second?" When she answered in the affirmative, he lowered the phone and forwarded the picture. "Does this interest you?"

There were tears in the woman's voice when she answered. "Oh, yes, he's beautiful."

"Good. The package is available for pickup at my office

tomorrow at seven PM. The fee is seventy-five thousand, cash on delivery. Are those terms acceptable?"

"Yes, absolutely. Randy and I will see you then." She stopped as her voice broke. "Thank you, Mr. Stark, thank you."

He disconnected the call, shuffled everything back into the folder, and found himself staring, once again, at Jillian's picture. "And that's how it's done, Miss Rishi." Anger rose in him, and his fist came down on the picture. He'd find her. It was just a matter of time.

~

JILLIAN SPENT the morning settling into Karla McAlister's amazing RV. She'd been beyond tired the night before with the dregs of the headache still making its presence known at the base of her skull. The time between her initial entry into the RV and waking this morning was little more than a blur. But she could recall Karla's parting words quite clearly.

Make it your home.

Jillian had never been inside a travel trailer before. She hadn't known what to expect, but it hadn't been this. The bedroom she'd slept in held a queen-sized bed. A large closet took up the far end of the room, and windows lined the east and west walls, giving the small room an airy feel. From the bedroom, she stepped into a completely functional bathroom. She turned on the faucet in the compact shower. The room quickly filled with steam, and a hot shower moved to the top of her to-do list.

The two steps that led down from the bathroom echoed hollowly under her feet. A bit of exploration revealed a concealed storage area holding onions and potatoes. She moved into the compact kitchen and found the refrigerator and the cabinets full of the groceries Wesley had mentioned. How had she slept through all of this? She laid out a package of pork chops, excited to cook a real dinner for Wesley tonight, in a real kitchen.

The coffee maker still held half a pot of decaf. Jillian fixed another cup, carried it into the small living room, and went to stand by the front door. She moved the curtain aside and sipped as the wind blew. She could see the pond from here, the water gray, the surrounding grass a dull beige in the muted light of the winter morning. Little waves swept the surface of the water with each gust of wind, and she shivered, imagining what it would feel like if she opened the door.

Jillian leaned her head against the cool glass and closed her eyes. *Thank You, Father. All the prayers, all the worry, all the trust I tried to have but never did... I never thought we'd be blessed like this. You've provided us with a place of safety and friends who might be able to help us untangle part of this mess.*

The words of her prayer gave her pause. Was she ready to take that step? Her discussion with Wesley had come from a vacillating bravado. She'd meant every word, but... She winced as Hannah did a summersault and a small foot connected with a coffee-bloated bladder. Jillian rubbed her belly in an effort to soothe the baby.

"Easy there, girlfriend, I'm going to need that once you vacate."

Love and protectiveness rose up in Jillian. Could she do

it? Could she face authorities who might place her and Hannah in a position to be threatened by Newton Stark all over again?

Look around you, daughter, and trust Me.

Jillian gathered her courage and went back to the bedroom. She snatched up the phone and the card with hand-written numbers lying beside it. *Who should I call?* She made up her mind and entered the numbers before she lost her nerve. Her grip tightened with each unanswered ring.

"Hello."

"Terri, its Jillian." She bit her lip and rolled her shoulders in a physical effort to release the tension. "If you'll set up a meeting, Wesley and I would like to talk to the cop and the lawyer."

6

Jillian held Wesley's hand in a vice like grip as they drove through Garfield early Friday evening. Christmas decorations flashed by on both sides of the street. Normally the displays would have delighted her. Tonight, she paid them little attention.

She and Wesley were headed for another meeting around an unfamiliar table across from more strange faces. A few days ago, it had been dinner with four amazing women. Not this time, though. *The cop and the lawyer.* Her stomach twisted, and her hands grew clammy. She didn't mind telling their story again...was pretty sure Terri and her friends had shared the basics with the cop and the lawyer within an hour of her call yesterday.

I can't keep calling them that. She searched her memory for their names, but her brain, overloaded by pregnancy hormones and worry, refused to give them up. *The cop* and *the lawyer* would have to do for now. Her grip tightened when Wesley slowed the car at the end of a sparsely populated street and turned into a sweeping circular drive.

They were at Callie's house because there were no kids to distract from the conversation. It was literally outlined in white Christmas lights. The peak of the roof, the eaves, the corners, the windows, and the porch rail all twinkled in holiday welcome. The cheery lights almost distracted her from the six vehicles already parked in the drive. *Six?* Her heartbeat tripped faster.

Wesley disentangled his hand from hers, shifted the car into park, and turned off the ignition. "Nervous?"

Jillian wiped her hands on the legs of her sweatpants. "No," she answered. Maybe if she said it out loud, she'd believe it.

"Liar," Wesley said softly. He turned and faced her across the console. "We don't have to do this. I know why you think we do, but we still have time to bail on the whole thing."

Run again? That was becoming an unfortunate pattern in their life. She'd run from home, he'd fled the country, they'd run from Ohio. And every time they took off, things got worse instead of better. "That's not an option, Wesley. Yes, I'm scared, but I want Hannah to come into a world where she's safe. That's up to us." She pulled the zipper up on her oversize jacket, reached for the door latch, and braced for the slap of frigid air. "And we start now."

Wesley scooted from behind the wheel and hurried around to her side of the car. He had his hand out to assist her before she had both feet on the ground. *Assist?* More like pull her out like a crane moves a steel beam. The car sat too low to the ground, and Hannah was too bulky around her middle to move with anything resembling grace.

The door to the house swung open, and Callie stepped onto the porch. A tall bearded man stood right behind her, his hands resting on her shoulders. She chafed at her arms. "Hurry, you two, or this wind will freeze you where you stand."

Wesley guided her along the short walk, his arm firmly around what was left of her waist. When they reached the two steps, the other man stepped around Callie and offered Jillian his hand. She took it gratefully.

"Careful there," he said as he helped her navigate the steps.

Callie ushered everyone in and closed the door behind them. "Did you have any trouble finding us?" she asked Wesley.

"No. Your directions were great."

"Those were my directions, son," the other man said with a grin. He nodded toward Callie. "She's blond to the roots. I love her, but she doesn't navigate." He held out his hand. "I'm Callie's husband, Benton."

Callie sent her husband a look and laid a hand on Wesley's shoulder as he accepted the older man's hand. "Benton, this is Wesley Price and Jillian Rishi." She turned to her guests. "Everyone's in the dining room. We've got coffee, cocoa, and a few snacks. If you're warm enough, I can take your coats."

Wesley surrendered his jacket, but Jillian bundled hers closer. "I'll keep mine for a bit. You'd think I'd be hot with all this added weight, but once I get cold, it takes forever for me to warm up."

Callie's husband turned and headed down a short hall, and Callie motioned for them to follow him while she brought up the rear. *Is she afraid we'll change our minds and make a break for the door?* Jillian pushed the thought away as unworthy. In just two days, these women had been kind to her and Wesley in ways they'd never be able to repay. Nerves roiled in her stomach, but Jillian was determined to do the right thing.

Good intentions aside, the sight of the two strange men, one in a police uniform, the other in a suit and tie, tangled her feet in the doorway and threatened to suck the air from her lungs. They'd been running for so long, avoiding police, avoiding anybody in authority. The idea of voluntarily surrendering themselves...

We haven't done anything wrong, she reminded herself. There was nothing illegal about running from Newton Stark's plans to sell their child.

Wesley had entered ahead of her and couldn't have seen her fear. Nevertheless, he reached back and took her hand. The gesture bolstered her, and she moved into the homey yellow room. The deep breath she pulled in was laced with cinnamon and sugar. The tantalizing smells should have comforted her, but they didn't.

The soft murmur of conversation around the table disappeared as they entered. Callie put a hand on Jillian's back, scooted in behind her, and motioned to two empty chairs.

"Here you go, guys. What can I get you to drink?"

Trepidation worked better than any heater. Jillian felt a

bead of sweat form between her breasts. She slipped off her coat and hung it over the back of an empty chair. "Did you say you had cocoa? That sounds good."

"Cocoa for Jillian and Hannah. Wesley?"

"Hot chocolate is fine," he said.

"It's heating in the crockpot." Callie picked up an empty cup. "I need a refill. I'll be right back, and we can get started." She motioned to the table with her cup. "Help yourselves to the snacks." She exited through a white swinging door, and Jillian caught sight of kitchen appliances and cabinets in the other room.

Callie was back before they settled, placing steaming mugs of chocolate in front of them and fussing over the snacks.

"I wasn't sure what you'd like or if you'd have time to eat before you came this way. I made ham and cheese sliders and sugar cookies." She paused for a breath and pushed a big bowl across the table. "And we have chips."

"Callie, sit down and let them catch their breath," Benton said.

The words held no heat, but Jillian laid a hand on Callie's, touched by the woman's effort to put them at ease. "It's great, Callie, thank you." She picked up a sugar cookie slathered in pink frosting. "These are my favorite. I think I'll have dessert first."

Callie smiled as she took her seat. "Ignore me. I fuss when I'm nervous. Let me introduce you." She turned to the men, and Jillian's gaze followed. The cop was forty-something, sturdily built, with blue eyes and curly sandy hair. The lawyer appeared to be close to the same age, the more slender of the two. His eyes were also blue, but his hair, though equally curly, was several shades darker.

Callie motioned to the man in uniform. "This is Karla's son, Nicolas Black. He's a detective with the Garfield Police Department. Next to him is Pam's husband, Harrison Lake, Garfield's best attorney."

Harrison paused with his coffee halfway to his mouth and shot Callie a smile. "I don't know that I'd go that far."

Callie grinned over her own cup. "You aren't me."

To Jillian's right, Wesley acknowledged the men with a short nod. Jillian did her best to swallow her apprehension. "Nice to meet you both."

The conversation they'd interrupted with their arrival remained stalled. Even the women, whom Jillian had never seen speechless during her short acquaintance with them, had nothing to say. Everyone knew why they were there, but no one seemed to know how to start.

Jillian was down to the crumbs of her cookie when Nicolas Black cleared his throat.

He shoved his plate aside. "Wesley, Jillian, I know this is difficult for you, but we need to discuss your situation so that we can decide the best way to help you." He motioned to Harrison. "We've gotten the basics from Mom and her friends, but we do have some questions."

Harrison leaned forward. "And some assurances. What you've experienced makes me sick to my stomach. Private and open adoptions are building bridges of opportunity for birth and adoptive parents that didn't exist a few years ago. I want you to know that the scumbag you had the misfortune to stumble across isn't the norm." He paused, and Jillian squirmed under the scrutiny of his intense blue eyes.

"You haven't done anything wrong. You guys are the victims in this little scam. We want to make sure no one else is taken advantage of in the same way."

Jillian toyed with her fork and looked at Wesley from under her lashes. He nodded slightly, and she straightened in her seat. "How do you intend to do that?"

Nicolas sent her a conspiratorial smile. "I spent twenty years in the air force security police. I have retired friends all over the country, in every branch of law enforcement, including the FBI. I've made a few calls, told them that I might have some information they'd be interested in. They're waiting for me to get back with them."

"I've got a few friends in high places as well," Harrison added. "The legal community gets a lot of negative press, and this baby broker gives that some credence, but like I said, he's the exception, not the rule. We'll have all the resources we need to bring him down if you'll work with us."

"What do you need to know?" Her simple question restored life to the table. Questions were asked and answered, notes taken, and it seemed like everyone had something to offer when it came to formulating a plan.

There was discussion of taking Jillian back to Ohio to confront Newton Stark on his own turf. She'd wear a wire with the FBI at her beck and call.

Wesley shot that idea down with crossed arms and a single word. "Nope."

Terri volunteered to pose as an expectant mother. If she passed Harrison off as the baby's father, they could infiltrate his operation, figure out a way to gain access to his files, and pass what they learned along to the authorities.

Sometime during that discussion, Callie excused herself from the table. When she returned, she pierced the boisterous discussion with a loud whistle. Heads turned her way, and she slapped something down on the table. The crumpled flyer from the clinic lay beneath her splayed fingers.

"This is what we need to focus on, people." She picked up the piece of paper and passed it to Nicolas and Harrison. "We're trying to reinvent the wheel."

The assembly grew quiet while the men studied the flyer. "What do you have in mind?" Nicolas asked.

"This came in to the clinic a few days ago." Callie took her seat and addressed Harrison and Nicolas. "You two make your calls, get the plan in place. Once you give me the go ahead, I'll call the number on the flyer and tell them that I might have some information for them. If they have a means to trace the call, they can see the clinic info. That will lend credence to my story."

"Callie." Benton lowered his head into his hands. "I don't like—"

"The call won't even raise a red flag. Why would they send these out if they weren't looking for a response?" She patted Benton's back. "I won't give them any details, but if I haggle over the reward and play hard to get"—she shrugged—"we might be able to keep this creep off balance long enough for your federal and legal friends to do what they do best."

Benton looked at Callie with an incredulous expression. "But—"

"And the best part of the plan is that I never have to meet with him alone," Callie said, rubbing Benton's back.

"No woman in her right mind would arrange a meeting like this without consulting her concerned and greedy husband who insists on being right by her side."

Benton straightened, his face going from *no way* to *when can we start*. "I can be concerned and greedy for a piece of the action."

The cop and the lawyer looked at each other. Nicolas nodded. Harrison smiled.

"I like it," Harrison said.

Nicolas nodded his agreement. "Me too. But don't get too excited, Benton," he cautioned. "Even if the feds like it as well as we do, once Callie makes the call and convinces him that her claim is legit, that will likely be the end of her participation."

He turned to Jillian. "You'll need to give an official statement between now and then, and you'll probably have to testify if the case goes to trial. But given the court dockets, Hannah will be pushing her second birthday by the time this thing comes full circle. You two game?"

"I don't have to confront him?"

"He'll never even know you're in Garfield."

Jillian took Wesley's hand. "What do you think?"

Wesley faced the cop and the lawyer. When he spoke, emotion vibrated in his voice. "Do you know what it's like to love someone more than you love yourself?"

"I think we can both identify," Harrison said, taking Pam's hand in his.

Nicolas leaned forward on his elbows. "I know this isn't an easy decision, son, but you can trust us. There are exactly eleven people in Garfield who know about this, and

I'd trust any one of them with my life. We can put this guy away for a very long time if you help us."

Wesley was quiet for a long time. His thumb rubbed Jillian's knuckles while he worked it through. He closed his eyes and gave a single nod.

7

The next week passed by in a slow crawl of normal. Wesley went to work every day, his hours a little longer as Christmas approached. Jillian waited for him to come home at night. She waited for Hannah. She waited for news on the investigation. Waiting irked her. Patience might be a virtue, but this was a crash course, and she didn't like it.

The cold front pushed north, and the central Oklahoma weather turned mild. The secluded days gave Jillian ample opportunity to check out the area around the pond. She took long walks. Brittle winter grass and dead leaves crackled beneath her feet as she explored. She studied the huge, old trees that circled the clearing. They were nude for now, but she imagined them in the heat of summer, green and leafy, providing a curtain of isolation between the pond and the three-story white house belonging to her hosts just visible between the bare branches.

Except for the occasional evergreen, winter had leached

the color from the landscape, leaving behind nothing but browns and grays. The only entertainment was the pond. The clear water reflected the blue of the sky and played host to a constantly changing parade of ducks and geese. Occasionally a fish breached the surface, disappearing as suddenly as it came, but leaving the water rolling and lapping in its wake.

A weathered dock stretched twenty feet or so from the bank. On the days when the bright December sun inched the temperature up past fifty, she dragged a lawn chair to the edge, tucked a throw over her legs, and passed the time with a book. Winter in Ottawa Hills, Ohio, meant cold with an unrelieved capital C. Jillian soaked up the unaccustomed warmth like a sponge.

Hannah turned a lazy somersault and pulled Jillian back from her musing. She lowered the book and stretched the fabric of her shirt tight across her belly, smiling as her daughter's movements rippled the material. Was Hannah getting impatient too?

Earlier in the week, Callie had made good on her promise of medical care. She picked Jillian up and took her to the clinic for an after-hours visit with her boss, Norman Rayburn. After a thorough workup, he'd pronounced her and Hannah healthy, verified her due date as late December, and set up a second appointment for Monday.

Today was Saturday. Christmas was nine days away. Hannah should make her appearance in about two weeks. How much more time would pass before they were allowed to put the worry of Newton Stark behind them? Jillian leaned her head back and turned her face up to the sun. *Father, please let this mess be resolved by the time Hannah is born. We've made so many mistakes. I don't want Hannah to be the one paying for them. We made a lot of plans the other night, but I know You have one too. Help us find Your path out of the problems we created.*

She gathered everything up and walked back to the shore. She needed to get dinner ready. Wesley planned to be home early tonight, and they were going shopping. They'd stretched each dollar 'til it begged for mercy, managing to put a small amount aside. It was past time to make some arrangements for Hannah. The baby needed a place to sleep, diapers, and other odds and ends. Buying gifts for their baby would be their Christmas gift to each other this year.

With her mind focused on shopping and a mental list of baby needs, Jillian didn't hear the cars until they were almost up the ragged trail that passed for a driveway. She stopped and watched two cars park close to the trailer. Her heart leapt as Terri and her friends waved and emerged from the vehicles a few seconds later. Jillian hurried forward. If they were all four here, there must be news.

"Enjoying the sun?" Terri asked.

"Yes. To have days like this in December...it's amazing." Jillian studied the women, searching the four faces for a clue, finally forced to ask. "Has something happened?"

Callie shook her head. "No, we're still waiting. The wheels of justice can be agonizingly slow."

Jillian looked at Pam, and the woman's dark hair swung softly with the negative shake of her head. "If Harrison's heard anything, he isn't sharing."

Jillian's shoulders slumped as she slipped back into the endless limbo of waiting.

Karla moved forward and tucked a motherly arm around Jillian's shoulders. "I know it's hard, but try not to worry about it. There are a lot of things to coordinate on something like this. Nicolas is very good at what he does. I'm sure we'll hear something soon."

"Thanks, Karla. I'm just so anxious to have this done, and when I saw the four of you..." She straightened with a smile. "But regardless of why you're here, I'm glad you are. Shadow isn't much of a talker. I have tea in the fridge." She climbed the two steps to the front door. "Come on in."

Terri backtracked to her car, talking over her shoulder. "Well, we didn't bring news, but we didn't come empty-handed."

Jillian turned to watch as the four women bent back into the vehicles. When they emerged for the second time, each woman held an armful of brightly wrapped gifts. They approached Jillian with wide smiles.

She could only stare at them, shocked.

"If you'll open the door," Terri said, "we'll stack these inside."

Jillian jumped, released from her frozen position on the step. She opened the door and stepped aside. "What's all this?"

"It's a surprise baby shower," Terri answered, dumping her load on the table.

"Or a Christmas party," Callie added as she squeezed through the opening.

"Surprise," Pam said, maneuvering her load through the door. A clear plastic box of party cupcakes resting on top of the stack slipped off, and Jillian snatched them from the air.

"Oh...good save," Pam said.

Karla brought up the rear. "And what sort of party happens without gifts?"

Jillian closed the door behind the women, leaned back against it, and stared at the bright packages. The presents, some in pink wrapping and some in Christmas wrapping, overflowed the tiny kitchen table and piled up on the floor. The women were crowded together in the small space, watching her with wide smiles. "Guys, I...you didn't...I mean..." She slumped with tears stinging her eyes. "You've blessed us so much already. This is—"

"These are Hannah's angel gifts," Pam interrupted.

"What?"

Callie patted the seat next to her on the sofa. "Come sit."

Jillian settled herself on the empty cushion. The cupcakes rested in her lap.

"Do you remember what we told you about the day we found the angel?" Terri asked.

"That's a difficult story to forget."

Terri grinned. "When we shop for our angel kids, we buy each of them a toy, an outfit, and a winter coat and gloves."

Pam took up the explanation. "We decided that God wanted Hannah to be one of our angel kids this year."

Karla lifted her hands in a what-are-you-going-to-do gesture. "But we couldn't decide who Hannah's angel actually belonged to, since we all had our hands on it that day."

"So, we decided she belonged to all of us," Callie finished. She looked at the stack of gifts. "It's so easy to go overboard when shopping for a baby."

"So." Karla got to her feet and crossed to the cabinets above the compact stove. "I'll get some glasses, and you get that tea you mentioned. Pam can serve the cupcakes, and once we've had our snack, you can unwrap Hannah's gifts." She lined glasses up on the counter and sent Jillian a wink. "I don't think she'll mind if you do it for her, just this once."

Jillian filled the glasses in a daze. These women were a force to be reckoned with. She studied each from under her lashes, grateful they were on her side. She passed out glasses then sat with her own tea.

Pam handed her a cupcake. "Have you been feeling OK?" she asked. "No more headaches?"

"Just the one," Jillian answered. "I told Dr. Rayburn about it, and he gave me some sample medications to keep handy in case it happens again."

"Isn't he a sweet old teddy bear?" Terri peeled the paper off her snack and licked chocolate icing from her fingers. "He delivered all three of my babies. I'm glad we got done before he decided to retire."

"I liked him a lot." Jillian turned back to Callie. "Is he really planning to live on a houseboat once he retires?"

"Told you about that, did he?"

Jillian grinned. "Yep, and there was a smile as big as Lake Superior on his face."

"I'm not surprised. It's all he can talk about. Norman will be seventy-three this summer. He's been delivering babies for almost forty-five years. Now he wants to fish and read."

"More power to him," Karla said, wadding up the cupcake wrapper and her napkin. "He's earned the right to kick back for a while." She tossed the napkin into the trash can next to the sink and motioned to Jillian. "You about done? These gifts aren't going to open themselves."

Jillian studied the gifts. She didn't understand what drove these women, but curiosity was about to kill her. "Pass them this way."

Thirty minutes later, wrapping paper carpeted the floor and baby items covered the table. Boxes of diapers, stacks of blankets, tiny dresses, soft as silk sleepers, and a diaper bag to carry it in. All the necessities were accounted for as well. Bottles of oil, lotion, and shampoo, baby bottles and liners. Jillian peeked into the last box and drew out a stuffed teddy bear with a pink bow around its neck. "Ohh..." She wrapped it in a hug and closed her eyes when it began to play a lullaby. She'd managed to hold the tears at bay, but now they fell freely as the music tinkled into the room.

"How do I say thank you? Not just for the gifts, but for everything?" She ran a finger under her eyes. "I prayed for a miracle...but wow!"

Terri cleared her throat. "We have one more gift, and now's a good time since you're already crying." She pulled a card out of her purse and handed it across. "This is from our church."

Panic welled. "You told your church..."

Callie laid a hand on Jillian's arm. "All we said was that we knew someone who needed some help. They didn't need the particulars."

Jillian looked from one face to another and waited for her breathing to slow. She opened the envelope, pulled out the card, and studied the square of plastic tucked inside."

"That's for the things too big to bring to a shower,"

Karla told her. "You need a small crib, and a car seat, maybe a swing. There isn't a lot of room here, but you won't stay here forever."

"Buy what you need for now and save the rest for later," Callie said. "The card doesn't expire."

Jillian swallowed, unable to think of a thing to say. "How much is on here?"

"Seven hundred dollars," Pam supplied. "Happy baby and Merry Christmas."

~

NEWTON STARK PARKED behind his office, cut the engine, and climbed out of the car. He opened the back door. The baby girl slept peacefully, bundled in blankets, oblivious to the monumental meeting and life-altering decisions about to take place.

A second delivery this week meant a Saturday spent in the office, but he didn't mind. This was baby number one hundred—a milestone. She marked five years of adoptions, five years of careful planning and refinement of his methods, and five years without even a sniff in his direction by any authorities. Newton planned to celebrate this to the fullest. Too bad for the couple due in his office in thirty minutes, *the fullest* meant an additional twenty-five thousand if they wanted to walk out of his office with this little bundle of joy.

He released the straps of the car seat and wrestled it out of the car. The things were a confounded nuisance as far as he was concerned, but getting stopped by the Columbus

PD with an unsecured baby in the backseat didn't appeal to him either. Anyway, it was the cheapest model on the market and an expense he'd pass along to his clients at a *slightly* inflated rate.

He set the carrier behind his desk and opened the file. Mr. and Mrs. Amhurst smiled up at him from their application photo. She blond, he with a head full of jet black hair, both blue-eyed. They'd been married for fifteen years and had no children. The couple had come to Columbus six years ago. They were both teachers looking to adopt a baby girl. They had a healthy savings account thanks to some family money and a nice stock portfolio. *No problem paying my asking price.*

Newton's eyes slid to the second sheet of paper in the file. A police report alleging the sexual assault of a student by Mr. Amhurst. Stark smiled. He'd had to dig for that little jewel. Once in his possession, his fee went up by half.

The report, filed six years ago by the parents of a fifteen-year-old student in Niles, Michigan, accused Mr. Amhurst of improper advances during an after-school meeting. The charges were later dropped due to insufficient evidence when the girl and her family left town. Suspicious and unproven, but more than enough to keep them off any legitimate adoption list. Bad news for them, good news for him.

How does he still get teaching jobs? Newton dismissed the question. Not his problem. The only thing that mattered here was that Newton Stark had what they wanted, and if they wanted what he had, they'd pay his price or leave empty-handed. He didn't care either way. He had other files in his secret stash. He could have adoptive parents with willing checkbooks in here before dinnertime.

The baby made a noise, and Stark turned in his chair. She stretched, opened her eyes, and looked up at him, a perfect piece of merchandise. He waited to see if she was really awake. He hated to greet the perspective parents holding the infant. Allowing the mother to take the baby out of the carrier for an up-close inspection increased the illusion of ownership. The dewy-eyed pleading look on Mom's face when she held the baby close while staring at her husband was priceless. He considered his bank account with a smirk. *Well, maybe not priceless.*

While he watched the infant, her little lids drifted closed. Newton swiveled back to his desk, closed the folder, and glanced at the clock. Ten minutes 'til show time.

JILLIAN TOOK a step back and surveyed the small Christmas tree. There were three ornaments left in the box, and she couldn't decide if she needed them or not. While she pondered the finer points of tree trimming, grunts and groans filtered in from the other room and made her smile.

They'd gone shopping and come home with the trunk lid of their little car tied down around a crib and mattress. They'd found a car seat on sale and a few more baby things. Then, since they'd had a little extra, they'd splurged on a three-foot Christmas tree and a few decorations, and they'd even budgeted twenty-five dollars each to buy each other Christmas presents. Jillian eyed the wrapped package

Wesley'd placed under the tree before she'd hung the first ornament. Curiosity nagged at her, and her hand snaked forward. *Just a quick shake.*

"Ouch!"

Wesley's voice had her jerking her hand back. She whirled toward the bedroom. "Wesley?"

"I'm OK." He came down the two steps, dabbing blood from his finger with a washcloth. "I think I'm the least mechanical person I know. The screwdriver slipped out of the slot, and my hand got in the way. Crib's put together though."

Her gaze moved from Wesley to the room beyond, unsure if she should tend to his finger or look at the crib.

Wesley laughed. He made a small bow and swept his uninjured hand toward the bedroom. "Go ahead. I know you're dying to see."

Jillian rose to her tiptoes and brushed his cheek with a kiss on the way by. She stopped in the doorway with a gasp. The box had called it a *mini crib*. About a third smaller than the normal size, but Jillian had still had her doubts about the fit once Wesley had the pieces strewn over the limited space in the small bedroom. But now? Now it sat in the corner of the room, pristine and handy, hardly taking up any space. It seemed to be waiting for a new baby.

"Ohh..." Jillian moved forward and ran her hand over the satin wooden finish. "Oh, Wesley. This makes it so much more real somehow. We're going to have a baby."

Wesley came up behind her, wrapped his arms around her, and caressed her swollen middle. "I can't wait to meet her." He rested his chin on her shoulder. "Thank you," he whispered.

"For...?"

"For having faith in me after I let you down. I don't deserve either of you."

She leaned back into his embrace. "I—"

Her cell phone's ring interrupted her answer. "*Grandma got run over by a reindeer.*"

Jillian plucked the phone out of her pocket. "Hello?"

"Jillian, its Pam. I have news."

The words sent a flash of heat through her body. She turned in Wesley's arms and nodded to the bed. "I'm going to put it on speaker so Wesley can hear, OK?"

"Fine just tell me when you're ready."

Jillian sank to the edge of the bed with Wesley beside her. She thumbed a button and put the phone between them. "OK."

"Harrison just got a call from Nicolas. The feds have been digging around in Stark's business for a couple of days. They've had his office staked out, and they saw a couple go in today and come out with a baby."

"Oh no," Jillian said.

"They don't have anything on him just yet, but they're interested enough to take the next step. They'll be in town Wednesday morning. Since Callie already called the number on the flyer once, they agree that she should be the one to call again, but she'll have a script in front of her and an agent in the room. They need you there as well, in case Stark asks questions Callie might not have answers for."

Pam paused for a breath, and Jillian and Wesley looked at each other, grim and excited at the same time.

"It's a go," Pam said. "We're going to put that monster away."

8

J illian saw Terri's car bumping down the path late Wednesday afternoon. A combination of anticipation and nerves drove her out the door about fifteen seconds before Terri brought the car to a stop. Not long, but enough time for the frigid air to cut through her gloves and jacket like a knife. She cupped her hands and blew a warm breath over them. The weather was headed back towards winter in a vicious hurry. The temperature hovered around thirty, but the blustering wind made it feel more like ten or twelve. The weather app on the phone couldn't make up its mind about what would happen tomorrow, but the prediction of a rare white Christmas held steady.

Terri came to a stop, and Jillian slipped into the car and clicked the seatbelt home. She held out her hands to the heater vents, thankful when Terri dialed the warm air up to full blast.

"Girlfriend, you're going to freeze that baby to death. I would have waited for you to lock up."

"I'm fine, it was just a few seconds."

"Um hmm." Terri put the car in reverse, maneuvered a quick turnabout, and headed to town. "Are you ready for this?"

Am I? "Yes and no. I want it over with. This is the first solid step in making that happen. But meeting with the FBI...I'd be lying if I said I wasn't scared to death."

Terri's expression turned thoughtful as she drove. "I get that. I've never been involved with an investigation of this sort. With the exception of Nicolas, I guess none of us has, so it's easy to understand that working with federal agents might intimidate you. But there are a few things you need to keep in mind as this thing moves forward."

Jillian twisted her fingers in her lap and waited for Terri to continue.

"First of all, remember what Harrison said the other night. You haven't done anything wrong. You're the victim, plain and simple. Second, I don't think the feds have a lot of time to waste. They wouldn't be in little Garfield, Oklahoma if they didn't think they had a solid case. And last..." Terri paused at the point where the dirt road met the blacktop and reached over to pry Jillian's hands apart. She held one in a loose grip. "God's got this, and I know He's going to work it out. I really think He brought you to us so that we could help you." She smiled. "There's no other explanation for that silly paper angel."

Jillian's lips jerked up at the corners. "Spooked you pretty good, didn't it?"

"That's one way to put it."

Jillian took a deep breath and swallowed a ball of emotion wrapped in tears that she refused to shed. "My head says you're right, but my stomach is still tied up in knots. Would you pray with me?"

"Absolutely." Terri put the car in park, shifted in her seat, and clasped Jillian's other hand. She studied Jillian's face for a few seconds before she closed her eyes and bowed her head. "Father, I just want to thank You for Jillian and Wesley. They're in a difficult situation, but they're trying hard to do the right thing. We need direction this afternoon. Give the authorities the wisdom they need to bring this man to justice. Most of all, give Jillian peace. Help her rest in the assurance that You have everything under control. We love You, and we are so grateful that You loved us first. Your will, Father, not ours."

Terri squeezed Jillian's hands when she finished, and Jillian murmured a quiet "Amen."

"Better?"

"Much, thanks." She straightened in her seat as Terri turned back to the road. "Let's do this."

It was after hours when they arrived at the clinic where Callie worked, but cars jammed the parking lot, and just inside the door Jillian was met with a cacophony of noise. Three men wearing dark suits and efficient expressions bustled about, attending to one task or another. Harrison and Nicolas occupied a corner of the waiting room with Callie and Benton and two more official-looking strangers. Their conversation appeared intense but didn't carry to where Jillian stood. Pam and Karla crossed to the door. Their frowns shoved Jillian's nerves back into her throat.

"What's wrong?" she whispered.

Karla crossed her arms. "They won't let us play."

Jillian wrinkled her nose in confusion. "Play?"

"Listen," Karla clarified. "We wanted to listen to Callie's conversation with Stark, but the feds won't allow it." She stared at the group huddled in the corner. "They went into all sorts of legal mumbo jumbo but it all boils down to *no*."

Pam put an arm around Karla's shoulder. "Oh, Karla, be fair. They can't have a bunch of extra people in there. If one of us sneezed or hiccupped, he'd know something was up. They're only letting Benton in because Callie wouldn't lie."

"Lie about what?" Jillian asked.

Pam leaned in, her voice low. "They're going to have the call on speaker. You know how hollow that can sound. They wanted Callie to tell him up front that she had it on speaker so that her husband could hear." She grinned. "She refused to say it if he wasn't there."

The door behind Jillian opened, and Wesley stepped through. "Wow," he said, pulling up short just inside the door.

That single word was all he had time for. One of the suited men in the corner rose and motioned Callie, Benton, and Harrison through a door.

Nicolas came across the room with the other. "Jillian, Wesley, this is agent Rusty Knight. He's an old friend and one of the good guys. Rusty, this is Jillian Rishi and Wesley Price."

Agent Knight shook hands with them. "Good to meet both of you." He focused on Jillian. "Nicolas gave us a copy of your statement. There are some points we need to go over, but it's getting late. Ohio is an hour ahead of us. It's pushing seven there, but our surveillance tells us that Stark is still in his office." He motioned to the door at the end of the room. "Let's go back and get started. We can visit more afterwards."

Jillian grasped Wesley's hand and gave it a tight squeeze. The men led them back to a small records room. Shelves of patient files lined the walls, and the middle of the room boasted a large wooden table with several chairs. Equipment cluttered the surface. Jillian identified a phone and a recording device. The second agent sat in front of a computer, but nothing else looked familiar. Callie sat on the far side with Benton to her left and Harrison to her right. Agent Knight pulled out one of the closer chairs.

"Miss Rishi, sit here please, Mr. Price you can sit next to her." Knight and Nicolas took the remaining chairs. The agent indicated the man at the computer. "This is Agent Kirk. He'll be handling the electronics."

He paused and leaned forward. "Let me explain how we need this to work. Mrs. Stillman is going to call Newton Stark and tell him that she might know where his daughter is. We're going to have the phone on speaker so we can all hear. I can't stress enough the need for everyone to be quiet. No one makes a sound except Mr. and Mrs. Stillman. If we spook him, this thing gets a lot more complicated." He slid a legal pad and pen in front of Jillian. "We have no idea what he may ask for in the way of verification. If Mrs. Stillman gets stumped, don't speak. Write your answer down for her. I'll be doing the same if I think of a question we haven't already discussed."

He sat back with a deep breath and turned to Callie. "When you get him on the line, string him along about the reward. At some point, he's going to ask where you're calling from. Tell him."

"You're going to lead him right to us?" Wesley asked.

"Why lie?" the agent asked. "He can have that info sixty seconds after the call. Hedging will only make him suspicious."

Wesley sent Nicolas a hard stare. "You said he'd never know we were in Garfield." He grabbed Jillian's hand and rose half out of his seat. "We're out of here."

"Sit down and have some faith, will you?" Nicolas looked at Knight and received a slight nod in return. "We don't have all the details worked out, but I'll share what we do have."

Wesley sat back down but held Jillian's hand tightly.

"We have the warrants we need to search Stark's office and residence, but we don't want to give him any warning. Christmas is on Tuesday, and Stark's office is closed on Christmas Eve."

Wesley frowned. "What does that have to do with you practically pointing a neon sign to Garfield?"

"If Callie can convince him to get on a plane to OKC on Monday morning, Rusty's agents can have free access to his home and office without Stark having a clue. They can tear the place apart if they have to. Between crowded holiday airports and the way flights are routed these days, he'll be captive for six hours or so and won't even know it. If we find what we expect to find, there'll be a group of federal agents waiting to greet him when he gets off the plane in Oklahoma City."

Wesley glowered at the men seated around the table before turning to face Jillian. "Are you good with that? It sounds good, but if one thing goes wrong, he'll know right where to look for us."

Father, please... Jillian swallowed around the boulder of emotion clogging her throat. "I'm not even a little bit good with this situation, but we have to do it. We have to trust God to protect us and these men to do their jobs."

Knight looked around the table, seeming pleased with what he saw. "Are we ready then?" Knight asked. When everyone nodded, he motioned for Callie to make the call.

～

Newton Stark looked up from his desk. The world was black outside his windows, and his stomach growled. He folded away the file for a new birth mother, shoved it in with the rest, and turned the key with a smile. A new prego meant the promise of another healthy deposit in his expanding bank account. *I believe I'll celebrate.*

He gathered his things and reached for the doorknob. He frowned when the phone on his desk rang. He swore under his breath and stomped back to his desk. "Stark."

"Newton Stark?"

He frowned at the unfamiliar voice. "Yes."

The voice on the other end paused, and he heard a throat clear. "Umm...are you still looking for your daughter?"

The question sent Newton around his desk and into his chair. *At last!*

"Mr. Stark, are you there?"

"Yes," he barked into the phone. "Give me just a second." He retrieved Jillian's file and struggled to recover his calm at the same time. If this woman had the info he needed, she'd expect a grateful father, not an impatient tyrant. He took two deep breaths.

"I'm sorry. Your question took me by surprise. I'm... understandably anxious for news." He swallowed and injected some worry into his voice. "I didn't catch your name."

"You can call me Callie."

He frowned at the odd echo that accompanied her words. "Callie then. Please tell me that my baby girl is OK?"

A chuckle came from the other end of the connection. "We'll get to that, Mr. Stark. Before I pass along any information I *might* have, we'd like to discuss the reward."

Suspicion drew his brows together. "We?"

"Yes, my husband is here as well. I have the phone on speaker so we can both hear what you have to say."

Alarm bells jingled in his head. "I'm not comfortable with that."

"Then this conversation is over." A harsh male voice crackled over the line. "Hang up."

"But you said—"

"And now I'm saying hang up."

"Wait!" Newton put his head in his hand. *Stupid, greedy people.* "What do you want to know?"

"How much of a reward are you offering for our information?" Callie asked.

It all came down to money. *Is there no humanity left in the world?* "Two thousand dollars."

"Ten," the man said without hesitation.

"Ten?" Stark nearly strangled on the word. "Eight," he countered.

"Goodbye, Mr. Stark," the woman said. "I'll tell your daughter you said hello."

"Ten," he yelled. "But I need some information."

"I'm prepared to answer your questions," the woman, Callie said.

"Where are you calling from?"

"A little town in central Oklahoma, Garfield to be exact."

"And you found me how?"

"I work in an OB/GYN clinic. We received your flyer a few days ago."

Stark raised his eyebrows. At least the money he'd paid to the private investigators he'd hired hadn't been wasted. "How do I know you're legit? Anyone can make a phone call."

The laugh on the other end of the line startled him. "Well, I know she isn't your daughter, but I don't care much about that. Whatever's going on is between you and her. How can I convince you?"

Stark looked at the flier he'd shoved into her file, then at her information. He grinned. Jillian's middle name was nowhere on the flyer, and it was too unusual to simply pick out of the air. "Tell me her middle name."

Silence greeted his request, and he was just about to hang up when Callie spoke. "Anila."

Stark's eyes closed, and his free hand clenched into a fist. "Give me an address."

"Let's not get hasty, Mr. Stark. If I give you her location, you might be tempted to cheat me out of my money. I assume you have my number on caller ID."

"Of course."

"Then what I'll do instead is tell you that she has another appointment at our clinic on the twenty-fourth. Why don't you book a flight and call me when you get here?"

The line went dead, and Newton slammed it back into the cradle. "Blasted woman!" He took a deep breath and let the knowledge that he had Jillian soothe his anger. Yes, he had her, and by everything holy, when he got her back, he was tempted to chain her to a bed and find a way to get a second baby out of her for all the trouble and expense she'd caused.

9

Stark threw clothes and toiletries into a small bag Monday morning. Christmas Eve...who took a business trip on Christmas Eve? He glanced at the dark outside his window. And if they did plan such a trip, who planned to be at the airport at the butt crack of dawn?

That woman better not be jerking me around. He paused his mental tirade long enough to align Jillian next to Callie. Swear words hung in the air of his bedroom for several seconds. If either of those women crossed him today... He jerked the zipper shut with a violent yank and let the thought trail off, his sleep-deprived brain unable to come up with dire enough consequences.

He shrugged into a coat, still fuming. Every attempt to call the woman back had gone unanswered. She was playing hardball with him and that irked him. Newton Stark didn't swing at the pitches, he threw them. He left the house, slamming the door so hard the windows rattled in their frames. A blast of cold air drove him back a step.

Stupid woman! Would it have been too much to ask to move this meeting up a couple of days? Days when it wasn't expected to snow in central Oklahoma. No telling what the weather would be like this afternoon when he landed at Will Rogers. *Afternoon.* The word tossed gasoline on to the fire of his temper. You couldn't just go anywhere in a straight line these days...no. You had to fly all over the danged country. The need to cross over Oklahoma completely, land in Dallas, and then come back to Oklahoma City made no sense.

He clicked the locks open on his Lincoln, threw the bag across the console to the passenger seat, and turned the key in the ignition.

~

RUSTY KNIGHT SAT in his car outside Newton Stark's office, sipping coffee and waiting for his cell phone to ring. The office was located in one of those trendy new professional buildings that seemed to pop up in the suburbs like weeds in a neglected garden. The single-story red brick building boasted lots of windows, spacious waiting areas, and plenty of parking. In addition to Stark's law firm, this one housed another lawyer, an accounting firm, and an interior designer. The street out front was quiet for now, but that wouldn't last. By the time the sun rose in the frosty eastern sky, the streets would be alive in a Christmas Eve frenzy as last-minute shoppers hurried from place to place in a bid to find Christmas gifts any sane person would have purchased weeks ago.

Rusty peered through the gloom. He couldn't see the other two cars, but he knew they were there, lying low, cloaked by darkness, and awaiting his signal that Newton Stark was in the air. He twisted the cup in his hands. His fingers itched to get into that office and tear the place apart. As far as he was concerned, predators like Stark deserved no mercy.

Knight was a proponent of adoption, he had two adopted sons, but they'd joined his family through the proper channels, with all the checks and balances in place. That included precautions to assure that the boys were placed with solid families, and just as important to his way of thinking, safeguards that kept families from being taken advantage of.

He brushed the screen of his phone and brought the clock to life. Six-fifteen, if the flight departed on time... The phone lit up in his hand with an incoming call.

"Knight."

"It's a good day for a take down," Agent Melissa Brant said on the other end of the connection. "And miracles abound. The plane got off the ground five minutes early. Mr. Stark is a captive audience at thirty-thousand feet. He's scheduled to arrive in Dallas in three hours, where he has a two-hour layover. There will be agents at the gate to keep tabs on him. Y'all have fun."

"Thanks, Melissa." He snapped the phone closed and glanced at the slowly brightening horizon. *Showtime.*

~

JILLIAN SNUGGLED into Wesley's arms and accepted his goodbye kiss. It might be Christmas Eve, and it might be that beyond Garfield, things were happening to change the course of their lives, but it was all-hands-on-deck at the discount department store where Wesley worked. At least the fast food restaurant that employed him in the evenings planned to close early tonight and didn't need him. He'd be home by six.

She pushed out of his embrace and reached up to pull the stocking cap just a little lower over his ears. "It's vicious outside."

He grunted. "And predicted to get worse before it gets better."

She thought of him hauling shopping carts from the lot to the store. "I hate it that you have to be in and out so much today. Stay warm, OK?"

He studied her with worry clouded eyes. "And I hate it that I have to leave you alone today of all days. Promise me that you'll stay inside and keep the doors locked."

Jillian drew in a deep breath and forced a smile she didn't completely feel. "I will." She brushed her fingers along his jawline. "Don't worry about me. You heard what Detective Black said when he called a few minutes ago. Stark is on a plane headed for Dallas. Go do what you have to do. Callie and Pam are coming over later to keep me company. It's..." A flash of pain stole her words. She sucked in a breath.

"What...?"

"Backache," she told him, waving him to the door with one hand while the other rested on her abdomen. "Miss Hannah is having her very own Christmas Eve party in there." Her lips twitched up in a smile. *Do I look as tired as I feel?* "If I can get you out the door and her calmed down, there's a serious nap on my to-do list."

He picked up his lunch and reached for the door, but the intensity in his expression didn't lessen. "I'll call you every time I get a break."

"I'll be here."

As if afraid she'd forget, Wesley turned the lock and wiggled the knob before he closed the door. Jillian watched out the small window as he battled the gusty wind out to the car. She looked up at the sky, heavy with pewter gray clouds, and shivered. The snow, a predicted four to six inches, wasn't expected to start before midafternoon.

A fresh spasm of pain gripped the muscles in her lower back. She leaned her head against the cool glass, rubbed the spot with both hands, and whispered to her unborn daughter, "Carrying you around is going to kill me before the next week is over." Jillian straightened. A nap sounded like a very good thing.

SIX FEDERAL AGENTS flooded into Newton Stark's suite of offices and fanned out. They skipped the spacious waiting room with its array of comfortable chairs and the small area, fenced off by privacy screens where the secretary probably sat, and moved to examine the two halls that branched off from there. The doors along one opened to a copy room, a small kitchen, and the restrooms. The shorter emptied into a large room arranged into three work cubicles with doors leading to two private offices along the back wall. On the right, the door was labeled Austin Fletcher. Fletcher was Stark's assistant. His compliance or guilt in the alleged crime had not yet been determined.

Rusty looked at the door on the left and smiled. He'd been waiting for a week for this opportunity, and he'd search Stark's office on his own. He motioned without turning around. "Hill, take the secretary's desk and the copy room. Kramer and West, Fletcher's office. The rest of you, go through these cubicles. I want every piece of paper scrutinized. I want the copier log examined and the computer files accessed."

The others hurried to their tasks, and Rusty ignored the movement behind him. If there was anything to be found, they'd find it. He crossed to Stark's office door and inserted the tool that would gain him access.

JILLIAN OPENED her eyes to the noise of pounding. She sat up, disoriented and blinking in the soft light. It was nearly ten according to the bedside clock. Her fitful nap had lasted almost two hours. She jerked to attention as the pounding continued. *The door.*

She struggled to her feet and winced in pain. The nap hadn't helped her back. If anything, it ached more. Her weary sigh trailed behind her as she waddled to the other room. She was so sick and tired of being sick and tired.

When she peeked out the window she saw four

women huddled in front of the door in a briskly falling snow. *Looks like we're a go for that white Christmas.* The thought made her smile as she pulled the door open and stepped back to allow her friends entry.

"Sorry," she said as they crowded into the room. "I was sleeping and didn't hear you."

"Sorry we woke you," Pam answered. "We were about to call 911."

Jillian rubbed a hand in a circular motion over her distended belly. "Hannah's keeping me up nights." She put her hands on her hips and studied the group pf women. "Are we having another party?"

Terri smiled. "Not really, but this promises to be an eventful day, and waiting for news alone is so tedious." She held up a sack with golden arches emblazoned on the side. "And we brought food."

Callie shrugged out of her coat. "Merciful heavens, it's cold. Coffee?" she asked, her voice hopeful.

"That's a heavenly idea." Karla shuffled into the kitchen. "I'll make it."

"Guys." Jillian frowned at them. She'd expected Callie and Pam but... "It's Christmas Eve. Don't you guys have better things to—"

"It's all good," Callie assured her, taking a seat on the small sofa. "We're having Christmas at my daughter's house tomorrow, and my baking is done." She patted the seat. "Now come sit down. You look worn out."

Karla flipped the switch on the coffee pot. "I'm good too. Kate and Samantha got back Friday night, and once Terri and I explained the situation to them, they volunteered to take over preparation for our celebration tonight. Between them and Bridgett, I'd just be in the way."

Jillian looked at Pam.

Pam grimaced. "I got a lot done this weekend too. I left Jeremy and Megan arguing over a short list of chores." She rolled her pecan-brown eyes. "I probably won't have a house left by the time I get home."

Jillian shook her head at her four visitors. "Make yourselves at home. I need to get dressed." She left them pawing through a box of DVDs and arguing about what to watch first. Jillian climbed up the two steps and closed the door to the bedroom. She sank onto the edge of the bed with a gasp as another spasm twisted through her lower back. Once it released her, she rummaged through the nightstand drawer for the pain reliever Callie's boss had given her. It wasn't a headache, but it was certainly the worst backache she'd ever had.

~

STARK FROWNED up at the departure board in the Dallas airport. He shook his head as the status of one flight after another was listed as delayed. He looked out the big windows of the terminal. Clouds but no snow.

He looked back to the board and frowned as his connecting flight into Will Rogers blinked from green to red. *Oh for the love of...* He gripped his bag, marched to the service desk, and, amid multiple objections, elbowed his way through the throng of disgruntled travelers. The attendant was on the phone, and Stark pounded the counter to get her attention. "What's the meaning of this?"

The harried clerk pushed hair out of her face and frowned before turning away. When she hung up the phone, she faced the crowd and motioned for quiet. "I'm sorry, but there's a serious weather pattern developing to our north. All flights into Oklahoma City, Tulsa, and Kansas City are subject to lengthy delays due to unexpectedly heavy snowfall." Groans met her announcement, and she sighed. "I'm sorry for the inconvenience, but if you'll be patient, we'll get you back in the air just as soon as it's safe to do so."

Stark pushed away from the counter. *I knew this was a bad idea from the get-go.* Well, he wouldn't let a little snow stop him. He was from Ohio, and they got more snow in one winter than these spoiled Southerners got in three. He looked up at the signs hanging from the ceiling and focused on the one directing a flood of passengers to the car rental desks. According to the GPS on his phone, Garfield was less than a three-hour drive from here. No way was he going to allow the threat of a little snow to keep him from bringing that girl to heel.

10

Rusty stood in the middle of Stark's office, his jaw clenched in frustration. The morning's search hadn't yielded a single thing that pointed to illegal adoptions. He turned in a small circle, his narrowed eyes searching the walls and the furniture. They'd moved every piece of furniture, gone through every drawer. *I'm missing something, but what?*

Weary from the early morning and the fruitless search, he crossed to the window. The sky was light now, the parking lot full. He leaned his head against the cold glass, hoping that the chill might snap his brain into action. His phone rang, and he leaned on the corner of a low credenza as he pulled it free. He frowned when the piece of furniture gave beneath his weight. He knelt to examine the floor while swiping the phone call open.

"Knight."

"Rowlings, sir. I'm at the Dallas airport, and we have a problem."

He sat back on his heels. "What sort of problem?"

"We lost Stark."

Rusty forgot his perusal of the floor. "What?" His free hand scrubbed down his face. "How?"

"The place is a madhouse, sir. There's some ugly weather ramping up north of here. Flights are being cancelled right and left, including Stark's. We had him at the gate, but we lost him in the press of stranded travelers."

"Rowlings, you find my suspect. I want a report every fifteen minutes." He disconnected the call without waiting for a response and returned to the floor. His fingers traced a slight indention in the carpet. *There's something under there.*

Rusty shoved the credenza away from the wall for the second time and gave the floor beneath a thorough examination. His fingers slipped into a second indentation hidden along the edge of the baseboard. He grinned when he pulled a section of the carpet away to reveal a large metal box slightly recessed into the floor. He replaced the flap of carpet, pressed the edges into place, and studied the spot. Nearly invisible if you didn't know it was there, and he wouldn't have found it if the cabinet hadn't been askew when he'd leaned on it.

He ripped the panel loose and went to work on the lock. Five minutes later the floor around him was littered with the evidence he'd looked for all morning.

His phone buzzed again. "Did you find my perp?"

"Not yet, sir. We tracked him to one of the car rental agencies. We know the make and model of the car he rented, and we figure he decided to drive to Oklahoma City when his flight got cancelled. We've issued a BOLO on the vehicle."

"You get back on the phone, Rowlings. We found what we were looking for. I want every cop in Texas and Oklahoma looking for Newton Stark."

~

JILLIAN TWISTED in her seat as the movie credits scrolled across the screen. Callie frowned at her.

"Are you all right? You've been fidgeting like a cat at a dog show all morning."

"I can't get comfortable. My back feels like it's twisted in knots. I took some pain medication before we started the movie, but it hasn't done any good. If anything, it's getting worse."

"Since when?" Callie asked.

"It kept me up all night. Why?"

"It could be labor."

"Oh, Callie," Terri said. "Leave her be. You thought the same about me, and I was fine. Sometimes a backache is just a backache."

Jillian put a hand on Callie's arm. "I'm fine, but I need to go to the restroom." She stood, took half a step, groaned, and doubled over. Water puddled on the floor at her feet.

Callie jumped up, steadied Jillian with an arm around her waist, and narrowed her eyes at Terri. "And sometimes a backache is more than a backache." She waited for Jillian to straighten. "Come on, let's get you cleaned up, and we'll drive to the hospital. Pam, go out and start your car."

Pam moved to do as instructed, but she paused at the open door. "Um...Callie..."

While Jillian and Callie turned to see what Pam needed, Karla's phone rang from the depths of her bag.

"It's Nicolas." She said and connected the call. "Tell me you have good news." Karla listened for a few seconds, her expression going grave. "OK, I'll let everyone know. Can you get a police car or an ambulance out here? Jillian's water just broke."

Jillian watched as the older woman nodded a couple of times. "I know you'll do your best, son." She closed the call and looked from Jillian to the others. "Nicolas said they found what they needed in Stark's office."

Jillian slumped into Callie's arm. 'Oh, thank God. They have him then?"

Karla bit her lip and shook her head. "He got away from them at the Dallas airport. They think he's probably headed to Garfield by car."

Karla's words took second place to the violent contraction that tore through Jillian's midsection. "They...oh..." She doubled over and her words came out in a strangled pant. "Oh...my...goodness."

Callie tightened her grip. "How long on that ambulance."

Karla shook her head. "A while. All of the emergency vehicles are digging out stranded cars or dealing with accidents. The snow—"

"That's what I was trying to tell you." Pam motioned out the door. "Everything's buried out there. I'd say at least six inches and coming down fast. We can make it to town, but it'll be slow going."

Jillian groaned again as fresh pain engulfed her.

"Let's get you up to the bed," Callie said once the contraction faded.

Jillian stumbled up the two steps to the bedroom and allowed Callie to help her back into the nightgown she'd changed out of earlier. She'd just reclined when she felt the pain building again. Callie pushed her knees up and raised the hem of the gown. She met Jillian's gaze with raised brows.

"You've got a very impatient daughter."

"I need to call Wesley."

"You need to relax between contractions," Callie said. "I can promise you Hannah will probably be here long before Wesley." She lowered the gown and stepped to the door. "Ladies, we're having a baby. Karla, get Nicolas back on the phone and tell him to put a rush on that ambulance, then call Wesley. Terri, I need your help in here. Pam, we need warm water and all the towels you can find." The cat meowed at her feet. "And one of you come get the cat. We don't need him attending the birth."

Karla, her phone to her ear, snagged the cat. "Callie, have you ever delivered a baby?"

Callie lathered her hands and arms at the tiny bathroom sink. "No, but I have a secret weapon." She dried her hands on a clean towel, used the same towel to wipe down her phone, and dialed a number. "Norman, it's Callie. When was the last time you delivered a baby over the phone?"

~

NEWTON STARK DROVE NORTH on Interstate Thirty-Five surrounded by drivers who acted like they'd never seen snow in their pitiful lives. Traffic had come to a near stop for an hour between Marietta and Ardmore. He was moving now, but, according to the GPS app on his phone, he was still about a hundred miles south of his destination.

He whipped the rented four-wheel drive Jeep Liberty around a slower car and yelled at the driver as he passed. "If you can't drive that thing, park it!" It was already after three, and the light was fading faster than he was driving. He peered through the windshield, taking in the snow-laden clouds on the horizon and the never-ending flakes raining down on him. Stark pounded the steering wheel. "Stupid, stupid women!"

He zipped around three more slower vehicles and released a sigh of relief. The road opened in front of him, empty for as far as he could see. He mashed the gas pedal and brought his speed up to fifty. "Watch and learn, people. I was driving in snow before some of you were born."

Five minutes later, he topped a hill and swore at the line of brake lights that stretched ahead of him. He threw on his own brakes and swallowed hard when the back wheels of the jeep lost their traction. Despite the four-wheel drive, the Jeep slid toward a steep ditch, out of his control. The last thing he saw was the embankment rushing up to meet him.

~

JILLIAN COULDN'T BELIEVE this was happening.

"That was a good one." Terri blotted Jillian's forehead with a cool, damp cloth.

"You're doing great," Pam told her.

Jillian relaxed, closed her eyes, and collapsed against the women who supported her back—Terri on one side and Pam on the other.

In the narrow space at the foot of the bed, Karla paced with the phone to her ear. Husbands had been reassured, Nicolas had no news to share, and Wesley was somewhere on the road between the store and home.

Jillian tensed as another contraction started to build, doing her best to focus on Callie's voice where she knelt at the foot of the bed.

"Terri, Pam, prop her up. Jillian, I want you to push hard this time. Norman says Hannah's almost here."

Jillian squeezed her eyes shut and put everything she had into a mighty shove, gasping for breath when the pressure left her body like a cork out of a bottle. "Is—"

A baby's loud cry spilt the air, and the tears of five women joined in the celebration of a new life.

"Oh, Jillian, she's beautiful," Callie told her. She stood, and Jillian strained to see as Callie patted the baby dry with a clean towel. Finally, Callie rested the infant on Jillian's chest and tucked a blanket around them both. "Meet Hannah."

Jillian bundled the baby close and looked down into the clear blue eyes of her daughter. She ran a light finger across the curve of a delicate cheek, smiling when the little bow mouth made sucking motions in response to her touch. It seemed like hours before she tore her gaze away to look at the women standing in a clump at the foot of the bed.

"I don't have words," Jillian said.

"You don't need words," Terri told her.

Outside, the noise of a siren split the snowy quiet.

"I believe that's your chariot," Pam smiled.

Karla left the room and called back from the front door. "An ambulance, a police car, and a couple of pickups. The cavalry has arrived."

Jillian looked up when she heard Wesley's voice. "Where...?"

Karla must have pointed him in the right direction, because he was crouching next to the bed two seconds later. He brushed a strand of damp hair from her face. "I tried so hard to get here in time."

She looked into his dear, worried eyes. This man, barely a man, had become so much to her. For all the worries of the previous few months, she had no doubt he would always be by her side. "You're here now. Do you want to hold your daughter?" When he nodded, she shifted the baby into his arms and leaned on his shoulder, content in a way she'd never been in her life.

Both of the new parents looked up when a throat cleared in the doorway. Nicolas Black stood there, hat in hand, a smile on his face. "I've got some good news. The highway patrol just called. They found Newton Stark in a ditch south of Turner Falls. He has a nasty cut on his forehead and a nice shiny new pair of bracelets. He won't be bothering you ever again."

Jillian closed her eyes. "Thank you, Jesus," she whispered. "For our baby, for our friends, for this news." She looked up at Wesley. "We can be a family now."

Wesley smiled and handed the baby back to Jillian. "I

can't wait, but for now, we need to get you to the hospital. They can't get the gurney in here, so..." He scooped her and the baby off the bed and waited while Callie secured the blanket around them both. "Allow me."

He carried her from the room, and, as they walked past the tiny Christmas tree, a white paper angel fluttered in the breeze of their passing.

ALSO BY SHARON SROCK

The Women of Valley View series

Callie

Terri

Pam

Samantha

Kate

Karla

Hannah's Angel (a WOVV novella)

Mercie series

For Mercie's Sake

Begging for Mercie

All About Mercie

Sisters by Design series

Mac

Randy